THE WITCH-STONE GHOSTS

A MESSAGE FROM CHICKEN HOUSE

What happens when you can see ghosts – actually a lot of rather irritating ghosts – but never the one you *really* want to meet? And to top it off, your dad's last wish is to send you to some remote island where the locals are not all exactly welcoming. Luckily Autumn has The Dog and Mum . . . and at least one spirit that might help. Talented Emily Randall-Jones won our *Times*/Chicken House award for this clever, haunted mystery. Time to dive in and discover what young Autumn finds out about the island that's 'wrong to its bones'!

BARRY CUNNINGHAM
Publisher
Chicken House

*For Alison and Ken,
Welcome to Imber....*

THE WITCH-STONE GHOSTS

Emily Randall-Jones

Chicken House

2 Palmer Street, Frome, Somerset BA11 1DS
www.chickenhousebooks.com

Text © Emily Randall-Jones 2023

First published in Great Britain in 2023
Chicken House
2 Palmer Street
Frome, Somerset BA11 1DS
United Kingdom
www.chickenhousebooks.com

Chicken House/Scholastic Ireland, 89E Lagan Road, Dublin Industrial Estate,
Glasnevin, Dublin D11 HP5F, Republic of Ireland

Cover design and illustration by Micaela Alcaino
Typeset by Dorchester Typesetting Group Ltd
Printed in Great Britain by Clays, Elcograf S.p.A

FSC
www.fsc.org
MIX
Paper | Supporting
responsible forestry
FSC® C018072

1 3 5 7 9 10 8 6 4 2

British Library Cataloguing in Publication data available.

PB ISBN 978-1-915026-10-1
eISBN 978-1-915026-51-4

For Daisy and Bertie.
I'm proud every minute to be your mum.

1

If I'm honest, Autumn thought, *I'd quite like to be the same as everybody else.*

She was standing on an underground tube station platform with a gentleman in a top hat on one side of her and a woman in overalls on the other. They were talking at the same time, because both were competing for her attention.

Anyone alive watching Autumn would've seen a small twelve-year-old girl with large, sea-tinted eyes and wild dark curls stuffed under a mustard bobble hat. Anyone alive would have assumed Autumn was absorbed in her book, when in fact she'd read the same sentence forty-three times because Overalls Ghost was singing Second World War songs in her ear and Top Hat Ghost was moaning about King Edward VII.

A guttural roar and a flash of lights and the tube train rumbled through the tunnel. The carriage doors swept open with a *beep* and Autumn dashed nimbly inside, squeezing herself into a corner. The ghosts, unable to leave the station, chased the train the length of the platform as it departed, *swooshing* through waiting commuters and stone pillars until they stopped dead at an advert for skin cream.

Phew. There were too many passengers squashed together with bulky coats and bags for a ghost to reach her here. She briefly considered just going round on the tube all day instead of going to school, but they'd call Mum – again – and she'd have to make up a reason – again – and quite frankly it was easier to just show up and hope nobody noticed her.

The tube juddered. Stuffing the decoy book back into her school bag, Autumn pulled out a pen and brown notebook and scribbled as best she could without fully extending her elbows.

ARCHWAY TUBE STATION, SOUTHBOUND PLATFORM
- Overalls Ghost
- Top Hat Ghost

She decided to omit 'both told me to beware' because recently ghosts had loved telling her to beware. It was one of their things and hardly worth noting any more.

In the past six months she'd had to stop walking to school because of Wailing Park Ghost, stop getting the bus because of Conductor Ghost that kept asking for her ticket, and use a different tube station because Christian the Tufnell Park Ghost had been particularly noisy about the upcoming apocalypse. Granted, he was one of her usuals. But he'd been a lot chattier recently.

But it wouldn't get to her today. Today was special. She would go through anything to get to that evening, because *finally* Dad was coming home.

He'd been leading the West Country birding tours for over a month now. He'd never ventured as far as Devon or Cornwall before, and even though he'd stopped by a phone box once a week or so (Mum thought mobile phones sent information to the government and had banned them) – 'Wrynecks today, it's migration time!', 'Went to a pub with a well for a table!' – they'd not heard much and she missed the very bones of him. Tonight they were cycling to Hampstead Heath to spot barn owls by moonlight and eat sandwiches under the stars.

Dad was coming home.

She hugged that thought to her chest like a hot-water bottle.

2

The train pulled to a halt and Autumn scurried through the doors before any more spirits could waylay her. She was small and fast, like a tube mouse, and skittered through gaps in the crowd easily. Once she'd reached school, she leant on a wall to catch her breath and tightened her corduroy coat against the September chill.

'Good morning, Miss Albert!' A disembodied head poked through the bricks, craning forward as if a mermaid on a ship's bow. With a yell, Autumn stumbled backwards and collided with a tall boy from English class.

The boy snarled. 'Watch it, weirdo.'

'Get over yourself, mate,' she retorted. Or at least she would have done if she'd been braver. Instead, she murmured a meek, 'Terribly sorry. My fault,' to his back and watched him ignore her.

With a noise that sounded like an inhale, the ghost *swooshed* through the wall in a cloud of silver stars, the head now perched atop a body clad in dark pink trouser suit and kitten heels. She batted the stars away carelessly, as if discarding dust. 'Petal, I need a quick word.'

Autumn screwed up her nose against the sickly familiar tang of hairspray and printer ink. Curse these dead people. Her good mood was slipping through the cracks. 'Mrs Kaur, you know our deal.' She spoke through closed teeth, like a ventriloquist. Talking to herself had never been a good look. 'You stay away, and I actually pay attention in science.'

The school bell screamed, and a crowd of students ran giggling towards the rapidly closing gate. Offering the ghost an apologetic shrug, Autumn gripped her bag and backed away. 'Sorry. I don't do this any more.'

'Autumn Albert, I *must* speak with you.'

The chill in the air turned to ice. Autumn's breath became dragon smoke, every inch of her skin tingling as if kissed by frost. It seemed Mrs Kaur wouldn't be ignored. Not today.

'Fine,' hissed Autumn, swallowing the churn of nerves. 'You can have two minutes.' She beckoned the ghost into a nearby alley, and they ducked behind large bins that reeked of old bananas and teabags. The gentle *pitter-patter* of rain began to drop on to the lids, and the two regarded each other cautiously: one dead, one alive, both framed by rude graffiti and chipped bricks.

'Apologies.' Mrs Kaur adjusted her shoulder pads and looked embarrassed. 'I don't enjoy doing that. It's for posers and poltergeists, not biology teachers.'

'Don't worry,' Autumn sighed heavily, rummaging for her notebook. 'But school's started and my name's already mud, so what do you need from me?'

The ghost opened her mouth as if to say something, but instead fell silent and lifted a delicate hand to Autumn's face. They couldn't touch, of course, but for one moment Autumn almost felt the frozen pressure of ink-stained fingers. She stiffened.

'My dear girl.' Mrs Kaur's whisper was hard to hear above the London traffic. 'I need to tell you something, and you must remember it. Will you?'

'OK…'

To Autumn's dismay, Mrs Kaur's eyes filled with tears. It wasn't the first time she'd seen a dead person cry – there was that whole missed episode of *Star Trek* debacle – but it was the first time it shot an inexplicable ball of panic hurtling into her own chest.

'Petal.' Mrs Kaur appeared to struggle choosing each word. 'You are so loved. You must remember that. Keep strong and, whatever happens, remember you are loved.'

3

'Why?' The rain grew fiercer, soaking Autumn's skin and blurring her vision so that the ghost seemed translucent. 'What's going to happen?'

But Mrs Kaur just shook her head sadly, fading once again into silver stars that twisted and writhed like the tide in a storm, leaving Autumn with only an echo.

'*Beware.*'

A horrible, nauseous feeling rolled in Autumn's stomach as if she'd been reading in the back of the car, and it was with trembling arms that she pulled herself up to stand.

Yes, she thought. *Being like everybody else would be very nice indeed.*

Her head buzzed as she wobbled on to the street

and towards school, racing through all the excuses she'd already used.

I overslept.

My dog ate my tie.

What did she mean, 'remember you're loved'?

What's going to happen?

I lost my school bag.

Do I need to worry?

The school gate loomed and the bees in her brain grew louder as she saw who was waiting for her, beige tie flapping in the wind. Mr Wilson. Her living, breathing English teacher. She hated Mr Wilson. Most teachers ignored her and let her melt, chameleon-like, into the background, but Mr Wilson didn't.

'Miss Albert. Good.'

He's going to suspend me. It's finally happening. Maybe this is what Mrs Kaur meant. Maybe dead teachers have a weird sixth sense about these things.

Students gathered behind him, hungry for gossip, and Mr Wilson put a hand up to silence their chatter. Odd. He looked like he was shaking.

Keep strong, Autumn.

A familiar voice threw her off balance. 'Autumn,

where have you been? Why are you so late?'

From behind Mr Wilson, a rain-sprinkled figure appeared, dressed in a carer's tunic with hair tightly braided. The sick feeling in Autumn's stomach turned to cement. If Mum was here, she was definitely for the chop.

'I'm so sorry, Mum,' Autumn stuttered. 'I tried to get to school on time, I swear I did, please don't get mad, but . . .' It was then she noticed the red-rimmed eyes, the tight pale lips. 'Mum, are you OK?'

Mum made a funny noise, something between a choke and a gurgle, and told her that Dad wouldn't be coming home again.

And in that moment, Autumn's colourful world turned grey.

4

The chair was made of brown leather and tarnished gold, and studs poked into her leg like an animal trap.

Seemed about right. She was a rabbit, freshly skinned.

Two solicitors were poring over Dad's will: one with a Starbucks coffee, an iPad and a pulse, and the other with an ancient white wig, half-moon glasses and a pocket watch. The first ignored the second, because only Autumn could see him standing behind the desk, tutting. She did her coat up tighter against the ghost-freeze.

'Whoa. What? You're saying that Luke's forcing us to move?'

Mum's sharp tone jolted Autumn out of her

trance. Her American lilt had surfaced and that only came out when she was *really* mad.

'Poppycock,' murmured Pocket Watch, removing his glasses and cleaning them with his handkerchief. 'Complete lack of common decency.' Autumn forced herself not to look directly at him.

The female lawyer spoke over him, her earrings glinting. Her voice was nasal. 'That's correct, Ms Albert. Following his marine . . . *accident* . . . your husband has left you and your daughter his house on the island of Imber. It's situated in the Celtic Sea, just off the coast of Land's End.'

'Huh?' Mum's eyebrows were rocketing off her head. 'So, my husband was scared *pantless* of water . . . and then suddenly he dies in the middle of the ocean. And – oh no, wait, there's more – he owned a house, when we could barely afford to keep the heat on? Let alone actually have a *life*? Who keeps this many secrets?'

'Cool it, Mum,' said Autumn quietly, even though her own head was humming. Dad had told her everything. Dad had told her how to imitate a wood-pecker's drum, how to light a campfire, how to burp the alphabet. He hadn't told her about a hidden house or that he'd planned to send her there. Betrayal burnt in her gut.

'And we can't sell it?' Mum had turned puce.

'No,' droned the lawyer, sounding bored. 'As I have said, the clause *clearly* states that you must move to the property in order to take possession of its assets.' At Mum's blank look, the lawyer rolled her eyes and spoke again, slower and louder, as if addressing a confused puppy. 'You have to move there, or you don't get anything. I imagine he'd discussed this with you?'

'Yeah, you'd think, wouldn't you?'

Pocket Watch harrumphed. 'No tact. No refinement. That is not how you deliver news to a grieving widow. In my day, we had currant buns and smelling salts.'

Autumn dug her nails into her hands so hard that satisfying crescents appeared in her palms. She felt young and invisible.

'We won't leave London though, Mum?' she said in a smaller voice than she'd meant. It was safe here. Ish. She was learning how to avoid the ghosts, even the extra ones. Anxiety began to creep up on her like an old enemy and her heart quickened. Could she stick her head between her legs without looking bizarre?

Mum placed a hand on her arm. 'Honey, I don't think we have a whole load of choice.'

London was her life. The dark grey blanket of the Thames, the smoky-aired cafe with the fairy lights and *dolmades*, the library with its dog-eared books, her friends (OK, none of those), the vintage clothes market.

And what about Dad? Would she be leaving him behind too?

'Poor urchin. It'll be the workhouse for her.'

The ghost, F. K. Weltingham, according to the portrait that he was standing beneath, preened his moustache into the same walrus-like flick as his painting and glared at Autumn with something resembling pity.

And then she made her usual mistake: her eyes lingered on him a tad too long and suddenly it was too late to pretend she hadn't seen him.

Weltingham's head swung round so fast it nearly came off. 'You can see me? Pardon . . . *pardon* girl, you can see me? It's you, isn't it? You're she.' Autumn quickly averted her gaze and busied herself doing up her zip.

Weltingham snorted and ran heavily round the table. 'Please, if you can see me, please, I need to pass on a message about the new lawyer. About the will. It's terribly urgent, miss. Please . . .'

'Sorry,' Autumn mouthed, following Mum out of the office. The *cheek* that they kept plaguing her, even now. Didn't they understand? 'I can't help you. Any of you.'

'Miss, please, you *HAVE* to listen to us!'

Beware followed her into the hall.

5

When they got back to the flat, Mum was so angry that she kicked a cupboard and held aloft a bottle of olive oil like a champagne flute.

'Here's to you, Luke Albert. Man of mystery and secretive as ever, even in death. *Salut!*'

Autumn tugged at the peeling wallpaper. It didn't *feel* right; the idea that her warm, extraordinary bear of a dad had secrets this big.

'Mum, why didn't Dad tell us about any of this? Why go out on a boat in Penzance when he'd hated water? The house, and Im-Imber?'

The word was strange on her tongue.

Mum sighed and sat cross-legged on the kitchen floor. Greys were snaking through her dark curls and new wrinkles had appeared behind her tortoiseshell glasses. Even her dungarees looked too big, like she was shrivelling.

'Honestly, sweetheart, I don't know. You knew your dad. It was all *live in the moment, drink in the magic* with him. Kind of intoxicating, really; it's what I found so attractive.'

'Yuck, Mum.'

'Sorry. But seriously, don't be surprised that your dad kept things hidden. I knew like, *nothing* about his life before us. Starting fresh was something we had in common.' She sounded flat, like she'd gone over this in her head a million times. 'He insisted on taking my name when we married. I never met his family and never asked anything. Maybe I should've, but I figured he had a reason. I mean, you were at his funeral. Only us and the twitchers even bothered to show up.'

The empty pews in the church had hurt. Suddenly desperate to get away, Autumn left Mum mumbling angrily at the floor and sneaked upstairs. The Dog, their brown mongrel who smelt like old hay and true love, licked her hand and padded after her. Together, they swept through the door of coloured beads and collapsed on to Autumn's rug in a heap.

'Not a good day today, mutt,' Autumn murmured into his fur. 'Any ideas?' He looked at her with his deep, dark gaze and farted loudly.

'Brilliant. Thanks for that.'

The Dog trotted to the exposed chimney that ran through the middle of her attic room and woofed gently.

'I know.' Autumn ran her fingers through her own tangled mass of curls and, to her surprise, felt her hands shake. 'I know I've got to tell him we're leaving. Do I have to do it now?'

The Dog stared at her pointedly.

'Fine. Stinker.'

She kissed his snout and joined him at the chimney, counting three bricks up and two across until she found the one she was looking for. As always, the brick was bitter cold, strange in her sunny room. With practised ease she pulled it free, revealing a Victorian black-and-white playing card speckled with dust. The Jack of Hearts.

'Jack?' she whispered to the card. 'Are you there? Can I talk to you?'

Immediately, the air cooled. A faint *bang* came from the recesses of the chimney, as if someone had dropped a poker, and a coal-smudged boy appeared, his eyes white and wide beneath the dirt.

6

The Dog barked joyfully and turned round in circles at his feet.

'Whassit? Autumn?' The boy looked dazed for a moment, as if he'd been caught sleepwalking, then shook himself awake in a cloud of ash. 'Oh, *blow*! I was watching the footie at Mr Mazur's. Penalties, Autumn, *penalties*.' He jiggled back and forth on scruffy boots, a sockless toe poking out of one. 'Gis five minutes, will you?'

'Oh, sure!' Autumn's voice was unnaturally high, a smile on her face despite the sinking of her heart. She plonked herself back on to the rug. 'Totally understand. Take your time.'

Perhaps it was her tone, or the fact her grin was starting to wobble at the edges, but Jack halted mid-jiggle, patted The Dog's head and accompanied Autumn on the floor. Even now, it seemed bizarre that his ragged suit didn't leave coal stains where he sat.

'Bad day, treacle? You doing all right?'

'Yep. Abso-tootly.' Now he was here, she didn't know how to begin.

'Chum, when you put "tootly" on the end of words, I know you're fibbing.'

They fell into their old, comfortable silence, and Autumn took in the shape of him; his mop of blonde hair that stuck up in all directions, his jagged, broken nose and his obstinate chin. He'd been her first ghost. The first one she remembered, anyway; the first she'd mentioned to Mum and Dad.

There's no such thing as ghosts, Dad had growled. It was the only time she'd seen him angry. *Now stop talking about it.*

'So . . . day forty-two.' Jack eyed her and tilted his head towards hers. 'I still ain't seen him. Have you? I even checked the laundry room where he used to eat his secret cheese sandwiches.'

Her chin came perilously close to wobbling. *Not today. You haven't cried yet. Don't let it be today.* She couldn't look at him. It was unspeakable to admit that Dad still hadn't visited. That not even the slightest, smallest hint of him had appeared. The crushing irony that after twelve years of ghosts appearing unbidden, the only one she wanted wasn't there.

'I ain't gonna hark on about it, don't worry.' Jack paused, and the tube rumbled outside Autumn's sash window. 'But he'll show himself soon, chum, you bet your britches, and we'll be here waiting for him.'

The hard lump in Autumn's stomach turned to stone. 'See, Jack. That's the thing.'

He looked at her quizzically and the dread tasted like metal.

He's left us no choice, Mum had roared. *No life insurance, no family . . . can't afford rent on one salary . . . my stepmom's in Ohio, darned if I'm crawling back . . .*

'He's making us leave London. I've got to move to Imber – some island in the middle of nowhere.'

As soon as she spoke, the words had left her and were out in the world – which made the whole thing undeniable.

They had to go.

Jack recoiled as if wounded. He didn't respond, but instead yanked his cap over his head and jumped to his feet. This was his fixing stance, when he wanted to sort things out and solve conundrums because he couldn't do anything practical.

'Autumn?'

'Yes, Jack?'

'You ain't going nowhere. Your da'll fix this mess.' He stroked his chin. 'Most ghosties are usually where we died, ain't we? Lor' knows I don't sleep in a chimney for larks.'

The image of Dad's things, thick with sand and seaweed, flashed. Autumn pushed it away, burying it alongside the thousand things she'd try never to think about.

'You know me and Mum went down to Penzance the day we found out, so we could talk to the police and . . . stuff.' She shivered, unable to lose the memory of waiting rooms and Mum hiding behind sunglasses. 'I stood by the shore for three days. He's not where he drowned.'

She didn't reveal the other reason she'd refused to leave the sea. How much it drew her, despite what it had done. How transfixed she was. She couldn't understand it herself.

Jack threw his arms in the air and coal dust spiralled. 'Well, we know he ain't where he lived. And them's the two possibilities. So, what are we missing?' His eyes dropped to the playing card by Autumn's foot. ''Ere, what about that? The special-thingy-wotsit that belonged to the ghost, that calls us and lets us move around like my playing card does?'

'The talisman?'

'Yeah!' he yelled triumphantly. 'The tazzyman. You just ain't found it yet!'

'Jack . . .' She didn't tell him that she'd already tried everything in the flat; that she'd spent every night searching for the unique, electric sensation a talisman offered as it landed in her hand. The hope in his mucky, impish face was too much to bear.

'OK,' she said finally, because Jack clearly wanted to be helpful. 'Follow me. You know where it'd be.'

7

As he always did, The Dog raced ahead and darted to Dad's study door, rising on to his hind legs and keening. It wasn't his *there's a squirrel* whine, or even his *I want a sausage* growl, but a slow, chilling, high-pitched howl.

'Poor blighter.' Jack clicked his tongue in sympathy. 'He misses him and all, don't he?'

'Does he need a sausage?' yelled Mum from downstairs, muffled by booming bass on the record player. She'd cracked out her Fleetwood Mac vinyl. They had time.

'No, he's fine,' Autumn shouted back, trying to keep her voice even before lowering it to a whisper. 'He's not there, mutt. Do we have to do this every time?'

'You know I'm the only ghoul in this house aside from Cellar Ellen, and she never shows her face upstairs.' Jack looked nervous. 'You sure he ain't here?'

'Jack, his ghost is *not* there. The Dog's just slow to catch on.'

The door groaned on rusted hinges as she nudged it open and Dad's scent wrapped her in a warm blanket. Woodsmoke and tobacco. Dad had always smelt like fire, even when it was ninety degrees outside. Once, Autumn had asked him why. *October child*, he'd said.

Jack gulped loudly.

'You can't be scared of ghosts; you are one. Besides, he's not in the flat. We're just here to look for his talisman.'

She said it more for herself than him because she couldn't get her hopes up, and yet the temperature had dropped and the hairs on the back of her neck were prickling.

Maybe this time . . . ?

She yanked the light switch and it blinked a few times before the bulb sparked orange, hissed and died.

'Oh blimey,' Jack murmured.

'Ssh.'

The landing light cast a pale triangle on the jumbled box room where Dad had spent every spare hour planning his birding trips and tinkling on the banjo. Binoculars, journals, thermos flasks and camouflaged clothes were thrown together on wooden shelves alongside bird books with spines up and covers bent, like miniature tents. *Sacrilege*. The sea tiles he'd got at a jumble sale were glued to the back wall like blue-and-white mosaics, a mix of ocean scenes.

'Where shall we start?' Jack stood by her side.

'I'll go through the stuff and see if anything stands out. Can you be on Mum watch? She doesn't like this being disturbed.' She swept her curls into a knot and clambered on top of the desk, straining to reach the high shelves.

'Right-ho,' nodded Jack. He had one hand on The Dog, who was so rigid he could have been stuffed, and the other flew to the small knife he kept in his suit jacket.

Autumn combed the room meticulously, clasping each item in her hand as she went. With every object that brushed her skin, an old memory surfaced and scratched her like sandpaper. The second-hand telescope: sitting in a hide with a sandwich and soup, seeking dusky warblers. The creased map: being whisked out of bed at sunrise to chase down the elusive hen harrier. The jay feather that glittered a burnt blue: an afternoon in the forest, building dens and eating blackberries.

But none of them sparked her skin in the way it should, in the way Jack's playing card had. They were just things.

'There's nothing here.' She avoided Jack's pitying grimace as she leapt down on to the floorboards. 'Never mind. Onwards and upwards, and all that.' It was hard to stop the pressure building under her eyelids.

'I'm sorry, chum,' Jack said. 'Was worth a—' He stopped mid-sentence and squinted at the far end of the room.

8

'What is it?' Autumn followed Jack's gaze to Dad's wall of sea tiles. There was the sea monster breathing out waves of smoke. The fish hiding inside a shell. The seals barking at the sky. 'What are you looking at?'

Jack wrinkled his nose. 'Well, maybe I'm seeing things, but the white stuff round one of them tiles looks a different colour to me.'

The sealant round one, a tile brushed with the waves of a storm, did shine brighter than the others. It looked newer.

'I mean . . . maybe?' Autumn longed for her bed and the darkness of a blanket. 'What does it matter?' Above her head, the light bulb hummed.

'Well, with all the advanced learning I've done in

my many years on this earth, chum, I'd suggest that it was put on later than the others.' Jack's grin was cocky, his voice high with excitement. 'And, if that's the case, one would have to ask themselves *why*.'

Autumn remembered this tile. She'd always liked it, with the sea crashing through brick and stone, and hadn't questioned why her water-fearing Dad had hoarded these and squirrelled them away. Until now. 'OK. I'm going in.'

Her hands shook as she clawed at the grouting. 'It won't come loose. I need a chisel.' She grabbed one from Dad's tool kit. Jack and The Dog flanked her from both sides as she wrenched the tile away, their anticipation as hot as steam.

It fell to the ground with a *smash*.

'Well, I'll be . . .' Jack gave a low whistle. The Dog scratched at the broken ceramic, meeting the rhythm of Autumn's heartbeat.

A small hole was gouged in the wall. And there was something stuffed inside, exactly as Autumn had hidden the playing card.

'Like father, like daughter.' Jack grinned.

'Cripes, Jack, *look*.' Autumn reached inside and wrapped her fingers round a spherical object wrapped in paper. She unfolded it gingerly – the paper was fragile as a moth's wing – and a pebble landed on her palm.

'Blimey, what is that?' Jack's eyes shone.

Autumn held the stone between her thumb and forefinger. It was light grey and smooth, about the size of a clementine, and there was a perfect round hole right in the centre of it. She could see all the way through to the other side.

'I have no idea.'

There was no immediate shock of magic that a talisman usually gave – no comfortable sense of belonging. But as she peered through the hole, the tiniest hint of something danced at the back of her brain, something unearthly and low that burrowed into her spine and burnt her skin and made her hair stand on end. Singing.

Yo-ho-ho, heave, my lads, the iron, lads, pull it lads . . .

As quickly as it had started, it ended. She almost wondered if she'd heard it at all.

'What are you thinking, chum? Is this his tazzy-man?' Jack was by her side again, The Dog nibbling her toes. Autumn felt the cool roundness of the stone in her palm. Inside her belly, a firework fizzed.

'It doesn't exactly feel like a talisman,' she breathed. 'But Jack, I've got a weird sense this means *something*. I know he had his secrets, but what's this about?'

'Who knows, with your da and his ways?' Jack said. 'It could be anything. I dunno. What if, now he's gone, the universe is showing you who he is? Was.'

Autumn clutched the stone. 'How do you mean?'

Jack gave a sad laugh, as dry and cracked as the stripes of dirt on his skin. 'It must be hard, living a life of half-truths. Maybe you're finding these now, so he's not hiding anything any more. Maybe that's as close to his ghost as we're gonna get, and you just got to enjoy the parts of his soul he left behind.'

'That's a really nice thing to say,' Autumn said quietly. 'Enjoy the parts of his soul he left behind. Guess I've got to follow his breadcrumbs, right?'

Eyes locked on each other, they whispered the next word simultaneously as if uttering a magic spell.

'*Imber.*'

9

'Hon, it's half past seven,' Mum bellowed through the door. 'We're leaving in an hour. Get up, get up.'

Autumn dived out of bed, the last snatches of *the iron, lads, pull it lads* fading with the sunrise. For weeks she'd slept with Dad's stone by her heart, and each morning she'd woken with a sense of him being close by, a snatch of song. It made him feel alive again. It made *her* feel alive again.

She eyeballed her recent attire – black leggings with dark, oversized shirts – with a wrinkled nose. Too drab. Not suitable for new starts. For the first time in ages, she plumped for colour: a stripy jumper, red corduroy dungarees and boots painted with rainbows.

'You look nice.' Mum blinked over her coffee as Autumn appeared on the front step, carrying her rucksack. 'Here.' She tugged at the loose scarf in her hair and wrapped it round Autumn's own curls. 'Now you're like a colourful Rosie the Riveter.' Autumn rolled up her sleeve and flexed her bicep, and, to her surprise, Mum wheezed a faint laugh.

'You're more *you* today, somehow. Wish I could be me, too.' With a watery smile that meant she was about to break down, she put her coffee on the ground and disappeared inside, leaving Autumn alone with a chipped mug that said *Kiss me, I'm vegan*.

'All right, treacle?'

With a *crack*, Jack appeared on the step next to the boot jack, biting his lip and turning his cap over in his hands. He looked pasty and wrong in the glow of the midwinter sunrise, like a painting that had lost its hue.

'Hi, chum.' Autumn's throat was as dry as bark. 'Or should I say bye?'

From somewhere a siren bellowed, and school-children laughed. Black taxis rumbled past. There was more than enough noise to hold a secret conversation.

Autumn couldn't look at him; could only stare at

the tarnished iron of the boot jack. 'So, I need to say something.'

'I'm listening,' Jack said seriously.

'You know I'm not great at . . . sort of, expressing myself. Sorry in advance.' She kicked her boots on the stone step, scuffing the rainbows. 'I just wanted to tell you . . . you're my best friend.' Her eyelids itched and she pushed her thumbs into them. 'I know you're dead and that, but it's true.'

'Ain't going to cry are you, Autumn?' said Jack, his coal-streaked face turning beetroot red. 'That ain't like you.'

'Not on your nelly.'

'Got your notebook?'

She pointed to her rucksack. 'It's in my box of bits. But I won't need it. You're *sure* you don't want to come?'

This time it was Jack's turn to squirm. 'You know I want to, chum. I want to go adventuring with you more than I can say. But this is my home. I ain't known nothing else in nigh on two hundred years. And let's face it, you don't want a ghost around cramping your style.' He blew out his cheeks and made a trumpeting noise. 'Anyways. You thought about what you're going to do when you get there?'

'It's like you said, I'm holding on to the bits of his soul and I'm going with the flow. A new start.'

The old, anxious part of her was desperate to know what the holey stone signified, or if Imber would reveal any more of Dad's secrets. But his own words kept ringing in her ears.

One tree at a time, my love. Never think of the whole forest.

One step at a time.

'Autumn?' Jack fixed his cap firmly on his head, sending ghost-ash fluttering into the air. 'Do something for me? Don't go on trying to be like everybody else, all right? You ain't like everybody else – you're magic, and you're spiffing the way you are.'

'I'll try, Jack,' she answered, but her heart sank.

The chimney sweep nodded curtly. 'Well, there we go. By the by, you're my best friend too. Hell, you're my only friend. It's a blooming lonely business, being dead.' He tipped his head like he was bowing, waved, then disappeared, leaving a hole in Autumn's heart.

10

Blocky towers and flashing billboards gave way to fields of hay bales and dark, rugged cliff faces that reached to the sky. They'd driven in Mum's orange Fiat for hours, the boot stuffed to the gills with suitcases and bin bags. Their windows were rolled down to the setting sun, letting in a strong gust of fresh wind that pressed hair against their faces in the same matted brown. The Dog was horizontal in the back of the car, farting softly with every bump in the road.

Autumn nibbled at the raw skin at the edge of her nail and shifted in her seat. Going with the flow was tough. If only she were less jittery. Her chest was ablaze with all of it. Leaving Jack. Dad's secret life. Passing Penzance and going all the way to the end.

The last time they'd done part of this journey, they'd been greeted by the owner of the bed and breakfast where Dad had been staying. She'd held his banjo out like an offering.

'But . . . he hated water,' Mum had said, dazed. 'Why was he on a boat, alone? At night?'

'I'm sorry, hen,' the woman had mumbled. 'He got a letter. A puffin colony. Then he went out into the rain without his coat.'

'Of course,' Mum had sniffled. 'Of course, it was a stupid bird.'

Darkness fell quickly and they turned into what looked like an abandoned car park with an empty, unlit hut on the far side of it. It was sandwiched by crags half-covered with mist.

Autumn stuck her head out of the window and tasted the sharp tang of ocean salt. 'Where are we?'

In response, a horn wailed in the darkness, plaintive and mournful, and the ghostly shape of a small boat emerged through the rising mist.

'The port.' Mum slowed to a stop. 'Imber's a ferry ride away.'

They might have been at the edge of the world.

'Wet skies and wet feet,' Mum muttered. 'Why on earth did he want us to come here?'

Autumn breathed in and her heart flooded. Dad's presence was a swift on the breeze, darting in the dark, just out of reach.

As they drove past the hut and on to the ferry, Autumn caught sight of a pale-faced man waving them through, glassy-eyed and silent. Her first Cornish ghost. She'd learnt about Greek mythology and the River Styx at school. This guy looked like Charon, the ferryman of Hades, carrying the souls of the freshly dead.

Did that make Imber the Underworld?

11

'How many seasick dogs do you know?' Mum yelled over the roar of the boat's engine, as The Dog vomited for the third time. Autumn stood at a safe distance, keeping upright as the little ferry rocked back and forth against the waves. The shape of the mainland slowly disappeared behind them.

'Bye, London,' Autumn whispered. London was the place where, for her, life and death danced comfortably together, where ghosts weaved throughout a landscape of swirled murals and vibrant markets. It had been home. But Dad had found them another one.

'Hon, watch your feet, you're gonna get splashed.'

She shifted just in time to avoid The Dog's latest vomit spree. They were the only passengers on the boat, a sardine tin battling against the wind.

'I'm going to take him back to the car.' Mum lifted The Dog up and cradled him like a baby. 'He can sleep it off under his blanket. Come down when you're ready.'

Autumn bent down and kissed The Dog's snout. 'Love you, mutt,' she murmured in his ear. 'Keep well.' He whimpered in response.

She placed her hands on the painted metal of the railings, the shock stinging her skin, and closed her eyes. The air smelt like rain and fish, feeling both strange and heart-achingly familiar at the same time.

'There's a local legend round here, y'know.'

Ice slithered along the railing as the air grew colder. The pale ferryman was standing next to her.

'Imber isn't your *usual* place,' the ferryman continued, his growl dripping with a strong burr. 'No true Cornishman alights on its shores. It's not right. Wrong to its bones.'

He was thin, eyes set deep.

She should ignore him. She knew she should.

'Wrong how?' she whispered, unable to resist.

'Not for me to say,' he said. 'Not for me to say.' He turned his back on her and descended the stairs to the deck below, his salt-soaked hair the last thing to vanish.

The boat's horn howled again, and Autumn's head jerked upwards.

Ahead, veiled in a dark haze of rain, was an imposing mass of cliff and crag.

Imber.

Her stomach bubbles popped.

They drifted into a tiny harbour lit by lamp-glow, their beams smudgy with mist. As they got closer, she could see silhouettes of crooked cottages built into the cliff face.

What was left of Autumn's optimism melted into a pool of unease. A familiar song was floating on the wind. It was quiet at first, but as they drew nearer it grew louder and more insistent: voices calling from the island's alcoves.

Yo-ho-ho, heave, my lads, the iron, lads, pull it lads
Till it's taut, it's tautened, lads, then let the iron go.

The song from the stone. Why was it the same song from Dad's stone?

The rhythmic tune didn't offer the same comfort

it had at home. Perhaps it was the two cloaked figures standing on the harbour wall, holding up the lamps that lit the way. They stood stock-still, singing out their sea shanty to the rhythm of a single drum, and Autumn got the distinct impression they were staring directly at her.

Wrong to its bones.

Just what was she sailing into?

12

The lamplight disappeared beneath the horizon as they drove up the slipway, the song dying into silence behind them. The Dog was rigid, his floppy ears pressed flat against his head. Autumn stole a nervous glance at Mum, who was craning forward with her tongue poking out between her lips. Were the singers she'd seen ghosts? Or had Mum spotted them too?

'Hey, did you see that?' Mum yelled and waved cheerily through the windscreen. It was the sparkiest Autumn had seen her in ages. 'Singers!'

Phew. Not dead at least.

She clamped her hands together to stop them from shaking. She put the trembling down to moving nerves. That was all. Totally normal.

'West Country people like singing outside,' Mum said knowledgeably. 'Like those fishermen in Port Isaac that perform at the docks.' She shoved crumpled instructions into Autumn's lap. 'It's only a couple of minutes. Can you direct me? I don't want to wind up back in the Celtic Sea.'

Autumn flicked on the car light and squinted at the barely legible directions underneath a scribbled map.

'*Drive off the slipway. Follow the road up and round the island till you reach Brae's View. Road not made for cars – it's uneven.* Seriously, Mum?'

'I know, I know. London this isn't. She was sweet on the phone, though.'

'Who was?'

'Beth something? She phoned a couple of days ago. She's our new neighbour.' Mum cranked the wipers. 'Not used to this whole people-knowing-our-business thing, but hey, welcome to island life, I guess. Privacy is now a myth.'

They were plunged into blackness, broken only by the silver splash of rain on the windscreen and head-lights on the track. The car bumped up the steeply curved road, slowing to a stop by the words *Brae's View* carved into rock.

'Heavens to Betsy.' Mum whistled through her teeth as they got out. Their new home was one of two tucked into the cliff, which hung over the roofs. 'What do you think the chances are of that collapsing on us while we sleep?'

Autumn peered upwards. The road coiled up round the island like a snake. The pointed peak above was its open mouth and their house sat somewhere halfway down its belly.

The lash of waves against the cliffs was as loud as thunder and it was too dark to see much further than the wet ground beneath their feet. Autumn and Mum held each other to stop from slipping as they approached the cottages made of whitewashed stone. Smoke puffed from the first chimney, pooling in the small gap beneath the rock, and the window glowed orange with dancing shadows. Watchman's Cottage. The other house – *their* house – was dark. Closed up.

Isolated.

Autumn tightened her grip on The Dog's lead.

'Over here!' A silhouette was holding a torch,

waving at them. 'Sarah Albert, isn't it?'

'It is.'

'Beth Emlyn,' said the silhouette. 'We spoke on the phone.' As they drew closer, Autumn saw her: old and wrinkled with deep, splintered lines in her face like the estuaries of a river.

'Come on in! The kettle's on the hob.'

The kitchen was muddly and warm. China plates were covered with old receipts and coins, jars of chutney were piled like a house of cards. On the dresser, an old-fashioned phone sat next to a large, rusty key.

Paintings hung wonkily around the room. A boat. A lighthouse. A brown-haired Beth, unlined and youthful.

'I'll show you round next door tomorrow,' chattered Beth, ushering them to a sofa by the fireside. 'Stay here tonight, why not?'

Autumn clutched her coat, sticking close to Mum's side. She was still on edge.

'I won't disagree.' Mum looked grateful. 'I'm tuckered out.'

Beth handed them a teacup each.

'I've made it with oat milk,' she said proudly. 'You

48

said you were vegan. Vegans like oat milk, don't they?' She sat on the armchair next to them. 'Heavens, I'm just *so* glad to have neighbours. It's been abandoned for too long.'

'Abandoned—?' began Autumn curiously, but she was interrupted by a loud *bang* as the door swung open.

'Elizabeth, where's the dog?'

13

All three of them jumped out of their skin. Somebody was standing at the doorway: a giant of a man in a drenched checked shirt and knitted jumper. For a heart-stopping moment Autumn thought it was Dad, even with the greyer hair. Like Dad, he was taller than most; his neck was slightly bent under the ceiling, as if he were too big for the space. Like Dad, he seemed to bring the outdoors in.

Beth went to him, a doll by his side. He kissed her roughly on the cheek and she lit up.

'Darling, it's past ten. Have you been out walking all this time?' Beth asked the giant.

'Course I have. Headed back when the rain started, didn't I?' He looked down at his hands, tanned and mucky, and grinned. 'Couldn't find my net.'

Beth took his hands and stroked them tenderly. Clasped in one of them were a frayed dog collar and a sea urchin fossil. 'You've been combing the rock pools again. You're cold, Fred.'

'Aye.' He added the objects to a Kilner jar on the dresser. It was full of odd, jumbled objects. An eggcup. A paintbrush. A penny whistle. 'Treasures.'

'Sweetheart, this is Sarah and Autumn Albert. They're moving in next door.' Beth smiled, but Fred flinched and crossed his arms protectively across his chest. His gaze fell on Autumn, a grey cloud passing through his clear stare.

'I know you,' he said quietly. 'You shouldn't be here.'

Autumn felt as if icy water had been poured down her neck. 'I . . .'

'You don't belong here.' The flickering shadows from the fire danced behind him, and he seemed the size of a bear. 'It's tipping it down, haven't you noticed?' Fred's voice was low, heavy with suspicion.

Beth collapsed down on the armchair and stirred her tea so violently that the spoon scraped the china. 'Fred, no,' she snapped, and the spell was broken. Autumn found her breath again.

'The dog, Elizabeth,' he grumbled. 'I let Bracken out three hours ago and she's not come back.'

'She'll be fine, Fred.' Beth sounded exhausted. 'She knows how to get home.'

Distracted, Fred nodded at them and waved a tanned hand as he ducked through to the hall. 'Nice to meet you.'

Fred left, taking all the warmth out of the room. It had followed him into his land of wool, seaweed and small doorways.

Beth cleared her throat. Mum cleared hers too.

'You mentioned on the phone he's unwell,' Mum ventured. 'It's dementia, isn't it? I've seen it before.'

'Yes. It's progressing fast.'

'I'm so sorry.'

Autumn was only half listening. Her eyes had slid to where Fred had been. A young beagle was sitting on her hind legs, ears pricked. She must have sneaked in as Fred left. Autumn opened her mouth, about to point her out, but something stopped her. The kitchen had grown colder.

'Autumn, Bracken was his childhood dog,' said Beth. 'She died over seventy years ago.'

Cripes, that was close.

Her first Imber ghost. A wetter nose than she was used to.

Bracken padded towards Autumn and sniffed her shoe. The Dog curled his lips into a growl.

'I'm so sorry he spoke to you like that.'

Autumn wrenched her eyes from the beagle to find Beth leaning towards her with a furrowed brow. 'He didn't mean it. When people get old, sometimes their mind doesn't work as well as it used to. Sometimes Fred thinks he's just a boy. That's why he likes to look in the rock pools, because he did it when he was a child. Sometimes he forgets he's married to me. Sometimes he remembers everything, and life is normal. Just now he thought Bracken was still here, but she isn't. Do you understand?'

'I understand, Mrs Emlyn. I'm sorry.'

Beth pressed her mouth into a tight line and stirred her tea loudly. 'And of course you belong here, Autumn. We're here to look after you.'

Later that night, squeezed into the guest bed with Mum and The Dog, Autumn couldn't get warm. Despite the heat of two snoring bodies either side of her, she shivered, cold in her bones. Whenever sleep beckoned, she was haunted by the cloaked figures and the ferryman's words until it was easier to cling to Dad's pebble and just stay awake until sunrise.

Remember why you're here, she reminded herself, itching with exhaustion. *Breadcrumbs. A new start. Dad wouldn't have sent you anywhere bad.*

'I didn't get there in time!'

Autumn sat bolt upright, nearly cracking her head on a bookshelf. Fred's voice boomed through the ceiling.

'I tried. I really tried. I promise.'

His plaintive sobs tore into Autumn, but Beth shushed him, her voice slowed by sleep. 'It's all right, Fred. You made it. Everything is well.'

'Lie down, honey.' Mum yanked her arm groggily. 'It's not for us.'

Autumn reluctantly dropped her head to the pillow, straining to hear the odd word break through the ceiling.

'Left too late . . . the waves . . . too high . . . I moored the boat . . . I ran . . . I tried . . .'

'Darling . . .' soothed Beth, just as muffled. 'Don't . . . so many years . . . to bed.'

Silence fell again, the crash of the tide the only

sound in the darkness. Autumn lay wide awake and wondered where Fred's wandering mind had flown, far from cosy kitchens and twilight rock pools.

14

Autumn shoved the pillow over her face with a groan. She'd finally dropped off just as the gulls started to squawk. Morning in Imber brought piercing light and it took everything in her not to poke Mum in the ribs and wake her up too.

Autumn wasn't great without sleep.

When she shuffled bleary-eyed into the Emlyns' kitchen, Beth was bent over the stove.

'Good morning! How was your kip?' the old woman asked, too cheerfully, glancing at Fred reading by the fire. 'Nothing disturbed you, or . . . ?'

'Oh, nothing at all.' Autumn stared at the floor and wished Mum would hurry up. 'It was super quiet.'

Fred looked up from his newspaper, his deep laughter lines crinkling as he smiled warmly. 'Hallo, there. Do we have guests? You should have told me, Elizabeth. I would've worn a hat.' Bracken stretched out at his feet and The Dog snarled.

'This is Autumn, Fred. She's moving in next door.' Beth spoke as if they'd never met last night, although in a way, they hadn't. Fred rose from his armchair and crouched down in front of her, surprisingly agile for a man of his age, for he must have been over ninety, and even kneeling his grey head towered over her brown one.

Autumn scanned his face for some sign of last night's oddness, but Fred's expression was as open as an ocean. He took her hand and shook it firmly. He had the same grip as Dad.

'Autumn, eh?' Fred raised a bushy eyebrow. 'What a name. *Season of mists and mellow fruitfulness.* What do you know of gardening, young Autumn?'

'Not much I'm afraid, Mr Emlyn.'

'We'll get you learning.' His accent was broad, rising and falling like a song. 'Did y'know I'm a gardener at the big Hawthorn House for Lady Isolde? I'll wager she won't mind a young appren-tice.' At this, his eyes clouded and he shook his head. 'That is . . . I used to work there. Lady Isolde's dead

57

now. Course she is. Fool.' He retreated to his armchair and raised his newspaper so it covered his face.

Poor Fred, thought Autumn, watching his socked feet jiggling frantically by the fire. He was like a living ghost, halfway between one world and another.

A crooked wooden sign swung in the wind outside their cottage. Turnstone House. Autumn bit her nails, wrapped Dad's old jumper tightly round her body and tried to convince herself it was OK. The twists in her belly were just those old nerves refusing to go, nothing more. No matter that the white cottage was splattered with gull poop, its windows cracked and clouded, or that Beth's hands trembled as she pushed open the peeling blue door. Nothing to worry about.

'I did try to clear it up a little,' Beth said. 'But with all the rain – well, it's not in a wonderful way, I'm afraid.'

A strong wind slapped Autumn's face, encircling her like a whirlpool and weaving round her legs and shoulders.

From somewhere far away came the faint ringing of a bell.

Clang.

'Autumn, hey! You staying on the cliff all day? Don't you want to see your room?'

Clang.

Mum stood in the doorway, hands on hips. Beth was next to her looking uneasy and Fred lingered on the front step, glaring at the ocean with his fists clenched. It was like he was avoiding looking at the house altogether.

Swallowing down the lump in her throat, she gripped The Dog's lead and led him inside.

15

'Ready for Ghost Central, mutt? Place like this is their dream come true.' The Dog huffed, which Autumn took to mean *yes, of course, curly human*, and trotted by her side. Autumn braced herself for the inevitable flood of ghouls, stomping on the niggling hope that Dad might be one of them.

The air was stuffy with the smell of musty fabric and old wood, and damp grew into mushrooms in the corners.

'Eesh,' Mum whistled as she bobbed beneath a low beam. 'How long did you say it had been abandoned?'

'Oh, it's been empty for years.' Beth seemed suddenly fascinated by a smidge of dust on the kitchen table. 'We didn't get out of the Hawthorn

Estate much back then. No idea how your husband came to take possession of it.'

Autumn and The Dog poked their heads up the chimney, down the back of the sofa, inside cabinets and behind toilet cisterns, but there was nothing remarkable at all. Just battered beams, faded furniture, dusty paintings and lots and lots of woodworm. There was no frosty tinge to the air, nobody croaking her name from fireplaces or scratching inside the wardrobe.

'See any dead people?' Autumn whispered into The Dog's floppy ear.

The Dog sniffed, turned around in a circle and collapsed in a heap on worn floorboards.

'So, that's a no then?'

He wasn't wrong. In fact, the place felt hollow – as empty as a seashell. It was kind of a relief really, but also plain *weird*. She had yet to come across an old house that wasn't rammed to the rafters with needy ghosts.

And, of course, Dad wasn't there. He was never going to be. She knew that.

She looked out of the mucky window and saw Fred standing motionless in the burgeoning storm, his eyes far beyond the sea.

'Time to get him home,' Beth sighed, opening the door to a sudden chill and spatters of rain. 'By the by . . . it may be best not to ask the islanders about your husband. Liam, was it?'

'Luke. And why?' asked Mum.

'Ah, I'm just thinking of you both, and your grief. Mainlanders are the island celebrities. Folks round here will be peck-peck-pecking, wanting gossip. For your sake, it might be worth just keeping your heads down, so nobody needles you.' She produced an umbrella from her bag and opened it with a too-big smile. 'I'd get the stove on, Sarah. Storm's a-coming.' Linking her arm through Fred's, she guided him away. Autumn watched them go through the rain-smeared glass.

'So here we are, honey.' Mum reached a hand round her neck and ruffled her curls. 'You and me, M-Dog and A-Dog. And The Dog. It's time to start our new life.'

The two of them watched gulls shriek and dive over the water.

'Let's hope your dad brought us somewhere good.'

16

Two days later, and Mum was screaming at a slug.

'Why are you in my house? Why is your trail all over my shoes? YOU BELONG IN THE OUTSIDE.'

The rain hadn't let up for a moment since they'd moved in. *In fact,* Autumn mused, as she scrubbed the mould mushrooms from endless nooks, *it almost seems spiteful.* The constant battering of the roof tiles, the water seeping in through every cranny and hole until their feet grew damp – they were marooned in a ghostless cliff-house, warmed only by the stove and Dad's old jumpers. Even the staircase seemed Gothic, draped in an ancient runner rug and letting out a moan every time they trod on the bottom step. At least they'd strung up their festoon lights across the exposed brick of the fireplace and installed the record player. Made it look a bit less like a Charles Dickens novel.

By the time twilight started to fall, the torrent had dwindled to a drizzle and a warm glow of evening sun poked through the window dirt.

'Oh, *bleugh*.' Autumn tore at the twenty-third mushroom, the bleach making her nose sting. She cracked the window open and stuck her head out, drinking in the air in gulps. Now the rain had started to clear she could see steps cut into the rock, leading down towards the sea. 'Mum, can I go and explore? The fumes are making me see stars.'

'Uh, sure.' Mum deposited another slug out the front door and peered down the cliff on to the beach. 'But don't go too far, OK? Just down those steps, so I can see.'

Bundled outside in a gigantic jumper and coat, Autumn breathed in the scent of the sea and filled her nostrils with salt. The ocean stretched for *miles*. Halfway to the horizon, a large stone arch speared the water, grey and barnacled.

To the right of the beach below were shadowy caves. To the left, the harbour, where battered fishing boats swayed with the tide.

She could see a few other houses too. Some tucked into the cliffs, some balancing on the edge. Dirty white like hers, stark against the dark, moss-covered rock. Red-berried trees poked out from crevices between them and several more cliff steps led down from one ledge to another.

Autumn sucked the wind through her teeth and laughed in disbelief. She was definitely far from home. In fact, Imber seemed like another world. But more than that, it seemed *quiet*. No babbling of the dead, no constant low-level moaning or begging. The noise, the soundtrack to her whole life, had gone. And it felt brilliant.

This really is *a new start.*

'Autumn Albert, I presume?'

Autumn's stomach lurched. A pale horse had appeared on the cliff path. A hooded figure was astride it, a lamp held high in a long-fingered hand.

17

A thousand fractured thoughts played on fast forward as Autumn stared.

A ghost. Two ghosts. Buy one get one free.

I should have known. I shouldn't have relaxed.

Don't look at them.

She staggered backwards, grappling for the door handle.

The figure pulled at the horse's reins and lowered the lamp. 'Oh! Abject apologies, I must look somewhat alarming!'

On second hearing, its voice sounded like tinkling bells, not particularly terrifying at all, and it lifted its hand to peel off the hood elegantly. A girl – possibly a little older than Autumn – was beneath, with white-blonde hair and violet eyes turned down at the edges. She slid off the horse easily.

'I've made you some apple cake.' She reached into the folds of the cloak and produced a brown paper bag, dotted with raindrops.

'Er, wow. Thank you?' At least the girl was alive. Ghosts generally didn't branch out into baking.

'There's no eggs or milk in it. I know you're vegan.'

On the chest of her cloak, an emblem was sewn: two circles in gold thread, one inside the other. A sudden thought struck Autumn and she loosened her sweaty grip on the doorknob.

'Was that you . . . ? When we arrived on the island? The singing?'

The sky went from indigo to the murky colour of slate, and the girl glided closer. The bottom of her cloak brushed the track.

'It was, yes. My name is Lamorna Hawthorn. Myself and my father wished to greet you in the traditional manner. We sort of own this island, you see.' It should have sounded arrogant, but she didn't seem to be boasting. Simply stating a fact.

Autumn gripped Dad's stone, burning a hole in her pocket. 'Um . . . what did that song mean? Is it special, or . . . or anything?'

'Goodness, who knows?' Lamorna blinked long lashes. 'They're all ancient, the meanings lost throughout the years.'

'Oh. OK.'

Don't look disappointed. Look normal.

Lamorna flashed a million-watt smile. Her teeth were pearly white. 'I'm here because I wished to invite you and your mother to a party tomorrow evening. Would you like to come?'

The thought of a party and pretending she knew how to make conversation about cake or tennis or phones – wait, what did normal people talk about? – made Autumn's insides shrink with fear.

'Abso-tootly!' she said, and then promptly wished she hadn't. 'Although Mum'll probably say no, she's kind of shy . . .'

As if by magic, the door flung open to reveal Mum dressed in second-hand waterproofs, a half-asleep Dog on the lead.

'Say what? A party? We are *so* there!'

Autumn wondered if it was too late to hide in a cave.

'Simply marvellous!' Lamorna gifted them with a

beam the size of the ocean. 'I'll come a-calling tomorrow evening, at the beckoning of twilight.' She leapt back on to her horse with the grace of a gymnast. 'Good night, Alberts!' And with that, the sad-eyed girl and her horse retreated down the track, leaving a waft of rosewater behind them.

18

'Well, get us. The island's shiny new things.' Mum dumped another slug on to the path. 'So, I'm not hanging around to be overtaken by our Slug Overlords. Want company?'

Still unnerved, Autumn picked up The Dog and led them down the jagged steps, kicking up pebbles as they slipped and wobbled. The air quickly turned damp, raindrops falling from the clouds and trickling down the back of her neck. Beside her, Mum rolled her eyes through water-speckled glasses.

'Just one minute of sunshine, *please*.'

They reached the beach and Autumn's boots sank into wet sand. The ocean was growing blacker as the sun set and was so close that she could almost taste it on her tongue.

It hurt less than she'd expected, standing once more by the dark expanse of water. Listening to the familiar gasp of the tide that had accompanied the worst week of her life back in Penzance, waiting for a ghost that might never come.

'Honey, I know what you're doing.' A gentle arm was on her shoulder, a wet nose on her knee. 'But stop picturing it. Not again.'

'It's not that. I just want to understand.'

Why had Dad hated water so much? Even after everything, the sea filled her with wonder. How there was a whole world beneath the waves. How her skin tingled from the spit of the surf and how much like *home* it felt, even though this was only the second time in her life she'd even come close to it.

As if it understood, the tide rose and fell in time to her breath – in and out. She closed her eyes and imagined she was controlling it.

They trudged along the shore and the ocean air blasted through their ears. 'I just don't get why Dad would send us somewhere that's ninety per cent H2O when he wouldn't go near a puddle,' Autumn prattled through the wind. 'Or why he never told us about this. Or why . . .' She clutched the stone in her pocket and forced her mouth closed.

Keep your secrets close, Dad had said once, face hidden behind binoculars. *You never know who they'll hurt.*

'Hey.' Mum yanked her to a stop. Autumn looked down at the sand. 'I get you're never happy unless you're worrying about something, but mystery and magic was your dad's way. Just try to relax and go with the flow, like you did the day we left. Rosie the Riveter, remember? Because I'm trying *really* hard.'

The faint *clang* of the bell tolled. It jabbed at Autumn's head like a knitting needle.

Drink in the magic.

One tree at a time.

Just go with the flow.

If only she were better at it all.

'I'm trying Mum, really I am.'

They went back the way they came, up the steps towards their house, The Dog nestled into Autumn's armpit.

'That being said, we've definitely landed smack-bang in the apocalypse.' They reached the top, and Mum jabbed her thumb to fisherfolk in the harbour below, luminescent in bright yellow dungarees. They lifted sandbags from a sailing boat and piled them haphazardly at their feet.

Concern flitted across Mum's face. 'They're collecting sandbags? We didn't need sandbags in London.'

The Dog whimpered as a blast of cold air rumpled his fur, and Mum lifted him from Autumn's arms. 'It's time for his radio programme. You coming?'

'Um, sure,' Autumn said, distracted. A new figure had appeared on the beach, not too far from where they'd been. 'Give me two seconds.'

Mum shrugged and disappeared inside. Autumn peered down at the silhouette on the shore. A dark shawl whipped behind; arms were flung wide as if they were calling the sea into an embrace. Welcoming it home.

Somewhere in the depths of the night, the bell rang.

19

'Autumn! Lamorna Hawthorn's outside!'

So, she'd been true to her word. She'd come 'a-calling'.

Autumn raided her wardrobe and held two outfits in front of the grimy bedroom mirror: a yellow pinafore with green dinosaurs on it and camouflaged overalls that Dad had bought her for bird trips. She frowned at her reflection. Why couldn't she wear normal clothes?

They'd spent the day making the house look decent – Mum, The Dog and her. She'd done her best in her small, shabby room: laid her patchwork rug, pinned up the retro tube prints, organized her books by spine colour and hung the fork-and-spoon windchimes, but now it all just looked like a mess.

She bet most people her age had cream-coloured carpets and posters of bands and their rooms didn't look like an artist's bin bag had exploded.

'Twilight's nearly over! Get your butt down here!'

Annoyed at herself, she plumped for the pinafore and slipped Dad's stone in her pocket. It may not have been his talisman but it made him feel close, and she needed a bit of bravery today.

When they finally opened the door, Lamorna Hawthorn was smiling. Framed by the setting sun, she looked surprisingly average in a green V-neck and riding boots, her hair tied in a low ponytail.

'Good evening! I'm overjoyed to see you!' She seemed it too, and Autumn couldn't help but wonder why on earth someone would want to hang out with a weirdo, her mum and a farty dog.

Lamorna beckoned them out. The evening air was chilly and Autumn tightened the strings on her hood, squashing her head like a melon.

Before they could get very far, a giant shadow appeared at their feet and the booming voice of Fred called into the dusk.

'Lady Isolde!' He wore blue striped pyjamas, boots and a flat cap, which he tipped tersely in their direction, his face hard. 'Why do you come here? I've not forgotten to tend the lilies, not this time.' His forehead creased further. 'They're hardy, lilies. Despite what you lot do to 'em.'

'Er . . .' Lamorna looked thrown.

Bracken's hyper barks sounded from their kitchen. The Dog yelped in response and hid behind Autumn's legs.

'Fred!' Beth came bounding out of Watchman's Cottage, a toothbrush in one hand. 'My apologies, Lady Lamorna, Sarah, Autumn.' She slipped an arm round Fred's waist and guided him back towards the house.

'Please, don't worry,' Mum called in her old, calming voice. Autumn hadn't heard it for a while. 'Why don't I come over tomorrow and we'll have a chat. That OK, Beth?'

Beth nodded tensely.

'The storm is coming!' Fred boomed back over his shoulder, glaring at Autumn. 'You don't belong here.'

She reached for the stone in her pocket.

'Don't worry, Autumn,' Mum whispered in her ear. 'This happens. There's no storm, only rain. And he's not talking to you.'

'I know.' She wondered who it was meant for. Who he was seeing.

20

They climbed the track away from the sea. Twisting its way inland was a row of houses and shops, decorated with faded striped awnings and vines.

'This is Mordros Lane.' Lamorna led them to a whitewashed stone building almost hidden behind one of the red-berried trees. 'And this is The Sea Witch's Rest.' She knocked three times on an arched oak door, twice with her knuckles and once with her elbow. 'We stop here.'

'See? Who needs the city?' Mum teased under her breath. Autumn nudged her in the ribs.

The door, hinged with black iron, groaned open to a riot of noise and colour. Villagers gossiped, instruments twanged and metal goblets smacked on to a bar.

'Is this a pub?' Autumn asked, wondering how many dead soldiers or grey ladies would be drowning their sorrows in imaginary pints. They loved a good pub, did ghosts.

'Of sorts.' The edges of Lamorna's mouth rose.

They took a step into the warmth and, as if somebody had pressed pause, the entire room froze. Musicians halted mid-note, drinks hung mid-gulp and every single face turned to stare.

Maybe her dinosaur dress hadn't been the best choice.

'You guys!' Mum adopted her movie star grin. 'All this for us?'

Cripes, she is beyond embarrassing.

'Mainlanders! Felicitations!'

A short bald man pushed through the throng, decked out in a sage tartan suit and bow tie. His great bushy beard twitched as he smiled; two apples for cheeks.

'By tide and by moon, how utterly delicious it is to welcome you here!' He shook Mum's hand with vigorous enthusiasm and patted Autumn on the head. She cringed.

The jolly man's laugh was as warm as firelight.

'Lord Hawthorn, the custodian of this isle. It is my duty – nay, my *privilege* – to welcome Mainlanders into our island family. Although, I wonder if my daughter has got there first?' He clasped Lamorna's hand and clutched it to his heart, but she snatched it away fiercely.

'Father, must you insert yourself into *every* part of my life?'

Autumn flinched at her anger.

'Autumn is *my* friend. I would like something that you don't steamroll over.'

Lord Hawthorn's small grey eyes twinkled like Father Christmas. 'Ah, the curses of a pre-teen daughter. One must cleave entirely to her will.'

Mum snickered. Lamorna knitted her eyebrows together further.

'No matter; I shall admit defeat.' Lord Hawthorn twiddled his bow tie and waved at the band like a conductor. 'Come, join with our music! Let us play!'

Numerous voices parroted, 'Lady Lamorna! Mainlanders! Welcome!' and flagons were thrown high into the air in greeting. They stomped as the music kicked into gear once more, a joyful, frantic tune like one of Dad's. It felt nice. Familiar.

'You see?' Lamorna offered a charming smile and pointed to an empty pew by the fire. 'You're one of us now. Ms Albert, I'll lead you to the refreshments.'

'Don't worry, I'll be back,' Mum stage-whispered in Autumn's ear, before following Lamorna into the crowd.

Steam rose from Autumn's skin as she took off her fleece. The Dog turned in three circles and settled on the flagstone fireplace, whimpering in the heat.

'Can't see any ghouls here. You, mutt?' Autumn scanned the room, woody and cosy with anchors and ships' wheels hanging from high beams.

The air was toasty warm, without the slightest tinge of ice. Everyone seemed to be breathing. No legless pirates or howling smugglers to be seen.

There *were* the heads that turned to peek, narrowing their eyes as if they were sure they'd seen her before. There was also the silver-haired woman in the shadows, wearing a blue skirt and blood-red shawl and staring straight at Autumn. But no ghosts.

Across the bar, Mum swayed to the music. She always fit in anywhere, Mum, throwing herself full pelt into whatever situation she landed in. *That's her gift, Autumn*, Dad had murmured wistfully. *Belonging*.

Not for the first time, Autumn wished she had that gift instead of her own.

21

The Dog was already asleep, snoring in time to the music.

'Everyone's super alive here, aren't they, boy?' Autumn murmured. Maybe she could relax too. Just a little. She clutched Dad's stone in her pocket and tried to lower her shoulders.

A smoking flagon of something hot was placed in front of her.

'You simply *must* try this,' Lamorna urged, pink from the heat. 'Ginger and sea spice. Imber's own.'

Autumn took a sip and tasted warmth and woodsmoke, fire and air. 'Cripes, it's rather nice, that,' she managed through a mouthful of foam. 'In fact ...' She stopped herself. *Dad used to make this for me.* Her mind burst with memories of film projectors and blankets in the park, and Dad's special 'Fire Foam' drink steaming in a throwaway cup. She closed her eyes and breathed it in.

'And now,' the fiddler called, as the musicians reached the end of their song with a concertina flourish, 'pray gather your partners for "The Sea Witch's Curse".'

'Oh!' Lamorna squealed. 'Autumn, would you like to dance?'

'Er . . . no. I'll sit this one out. I'll watch you.'

'Very well. See you anon!' Lamorna skipped towards the band, where tables were pushed to the corner of the room and islanders gathered in the empty space.

The dancers stood in two lines, three on either side. The music swelled with the beat of a drum, and Lamorna and her partner joined hands and spun round, her white hair flying like a swan's wing. The group weaved round each other, in and out to the tune of the strings. One moment they were a circle, then a hexagon, a square and a six-pointed star – all the while taking small, loud steps and kicking their feet off the ground in a shuffle and a sweep.

It felt magical, being in the warmth while the

84

windows darkened. Autumn lowered her shoulders a bit more.

'And lo, my father ruins it all.' Lamorna huffed and sidled next to Autumn. Lord Hawthorn had placed himself in the middle of the dancers, twirling on the spot with a wide smile and arms in a circle above his head. 'Why are parents so sublimely embarrassing?'

'Sorry, you're asking *me*?' Autumn glared at Mum, animatedly talking about feminism to a random islander. 'I can't take her anywhere without this happening.'

The two girls giggled and Autumn felt a shock of warmth, a spark of connection. Was this what it was like, making a real-life, breathing friend? She had no idea: school had brought a big fat pile of nothing except loneliness, dead science teachers and jeers in the hallway.

'Is it just the two of you?' Lamorna asked, as the music ended with a roar of applause.

'And The Dog. My dad . . .' Autumn hadn't said it out loud yet. But there was a first time for everything. 'My dad died. A couple of months ago.'

There it was, out in the world. But it didn't hurt

to hear the words spoken. In fact, it made the lump in her throat a bit smaller.

Lamorna looked at Autumn with large, clear eyes. 'I'm *awfully* sorry.' It didn't sound false, or awkward. 'I know how you feel. My mother passed when I was ten. I miss her each moment.'

'I'm sorry too.'

'Life and death, Autumn. As natural as sea and sky. Alas, knowing that does not make it any easier.' Lamorna fiddled with her fingernails and Autumn felt a pang of pity.

Surely, she could ask Lamorna about Dad's stone? That would be safe, wouldn't it? The words bubbled and swam, desperate to tumble out of her mouth, but Beth's warning to Mum rang in her head like an alarm bell.

By the by . . . it may be best not to ask the islanders about your husband. For your sake, it might be worth just keeping your heads down.

Lamorna eyed her over the goblet. 'I know it may seem . . . different. My cloak, our way of speaking, the songs and what-have-you.'

Autumn shook her head too fiercely.

'But it's just what happens when you live in a place

like this. Tradition is our bread and butter, Autumn. But then, doesn't every place have its own eccentricities? Its own folklore?'

She hadn't thought of it like that. But of course, London had its brightly coloured carnivals, fireworks and burning Guys. Pearly Kings and Queens. The Changing of the Guard at Buckingham Place. Maybe things only seemed weird if you weren't used to them.

And hey, she was a girl who spoke to the dead, so what did she know about normal?

'D'ya know,' Autumn rested her chin on her hand with a wry smile, 'they say if the ravens ever leave the Tower of London the monarchy will fall?'

Lamorna laughed. It wasn't a tinkling one this time, but a big burst from her belly. 'See? Everywhere's strange. Even *we* don't believe that birds can control a country.'

Despite the strangeness of it all, Autumn felt a warm glow, like a firefly was dancing round her chest. Perhaps this was what it was like to feel accepted. To belong.

22

The night drew to a close, and Autumn and Mum were bustled to the door with 'farewell's echoing in their ears. Mum slid into the darkness first, with Autumn slowed by The Dog sniffing everyone's toes.

As she reached the door, the woman in the scarlet shawl emerged from the throng, green eyes locked on Autumn's own. She wore small, glistening jewels in her pinned silver hair, and bronze bangles snaked up her arm. She seemed ageless, her skin as clear as dew.

'Welcome to Imber, little maid.' Her voice was deep. Melodic. 'You are home now.'

Before Autumn could summon up the courage to speak, the woman nudged open the door and

Autumn was outside, the beamed ceiling now a sky full of stars. She nearly collided with a tree trunk.

'Come on, slowpoke,' Mum called. 'Quit the daze. Bed beckons.'

The chilly air bit as they trudged down Mordros Lane and Autumn had to skip to fight off the goosebumps.

Mum was attempting her own – embarrassing – version of the step dance. 'Oh, hon, don't you think we're going to *love* Imber? With the music and the *community*? Dad just brought us to the most perfect place. I feel like he's showing us his soul.'

Just like Jack said, Autumn thought with a smile.

Below their feet, white waves reared and crashed into the rocks. The mainland was far away, half-obscured by a low cloud. London and its myriad of ghosts was another world.

'I wonder where I can get dance lessons,' said Mum.

They reached Turnstone House and piled through the door in a heap, kicking off their wellies and coats. The Dog snuggled on the sofa with a grumble and a fart. Autumn listened to Mum sing as she put the kettle on the hob, and something clicked.

'Mum?' she ventured.

'Yeah, hon?'

'You're *you* again.'

Mum paused. She was trying not to blub, Autumn could tell.

'Oh, sweetheart,' she said, wiping her steamy glasses on her jumper. 'Not yet, I'm not. But I'm a lot closer than I was. You?'

'Yeah,' Autumn said, and squeezed the stone. 'Me too.'

It wasn't until she was lying in bed and watching her windchimes dance that she realized. She hadn't used her notebook in ages. It had been her lifeline in London, and now she couldn't remember the last time she'd even opened it. The last ghost she'd seen.

Curious, she pulled open her bedside drawer to find her box of bits at the back, stuffed with everything she didn't have a home for. She rifled through the blunt pencils, the random badges and ticket stubs from folk nights with Dad until she found it, sprinkled with newly laid dust.

The scent of something tickled her nose but she brushed it away without thinking. She heard The Dog racing up the stairs and he threw himself at the bed, scratching her arms with his claws.

'Down, mutt. What's up with you?'

She flicked through her notebook, scanning her own desperate scrawls about milkmaids with flashing eyes, town criers shrieking. She wondered if they missed her. Or if they'd even noticed.

The aroma grew stronger. The Dog leapt on to her bed and licked her hand, yelping sharply in her ear.

Hold on.

She knew that smell. It was the smell of coal dust.

Her heart in her mouth, she reached back into the drawer and tipped the box of bits upside down.

Lying beneath a beaded bracelet she'd made with Mum was a Victorian black-and-white playing card. The Jack of Hearts.

'Jack?' she whispered.

And in a flash of ash and light, somehow looking both ecstatic and sheepish, there he was.

23

'Jack!' Her mouth was suddenly full of sawdust. The old, icy sensation of him made her shiver. 'How ...? I left ...'

The Dog ran in manic circles round his ankles.

'The tazzyman in London, I know.' He chewed his lip. 'I swear blind, I didn't make this happen, Autumn. You know I didn't want to leave the house; it's my home. I dunno why I'm here.'

'Hold on ...'

But the words were falling out of him at super-speed. He stumbled over each one, refusing to meet her eye. 'I listened when you said you wanted to be like everybody else, honest I did.'

Autumn closed the door quietly, feeling fit to burst. Two worlds had suddenly crashed together, like shards of a broken mirror, and it was hard not to feel dizzy. On the other hand, *Jack*. He was her safe place. Wasn't he?

Jack fidgeted with his cap and backed towards the open window, forming a ghostly shadow against the darkening sky. He looked so vexed.

'I'll keep on hiding the whole time, I promise.' He eyed the hearth in her room, draped with her vine garland. 'How's the fireplace here – comfy?'

'Cripes, Jack, will you be quiet for one second? Mum must have packed the card. I'm really happy to see you. Honest.'

He was only ash and air but he was her home, and he was here – and he made the Dad-shaped hole in her close a bit.

But that firefly feeling. The lack of dead people. And the giggling with Lamorna. Tonight had been the first time in . . . well, a lifetime . . . that she'd felt anything resembling normal, and now here was the stark reminder that she wasn't. Not really.

She stuffed that nasty feeling deep inside her belly.

Jack cracked a smile so wide the edges of his mouth reached his eyes. 'Well, if you're happy, then

I'm cock-a-hoop.' He flopped on to her patchwork rug and ruffled The Dog's ears. Autumn's heart tugged at the familiar sight in a new room. He was out of place, like a puzzle piece that didn't fit. 'Tell me everything. What's been happening?'

She joined him on the rug and hugged her knees tightly to her chest. It all tumbled out: Fred and his moments, Lamorna, the pub, Imber's music and the song at the harbour – the same she'd heard through Dad's stone. Jack sat and listened silently until she was finished.

'But there are almost *no* ghosts here, Jack. Seriously, aside from a beagle, *you're it*.'

'Flaming marvellous!'

'Don't you think that's strange, though?'

He wrinkled his broken nose. 'P'rhaps. Can't say I'll be sorry not to run into any. I don't like ghosts.'

'You have mentioned that, yeah.'

'And nothing on your da?'

The guilt pricked like a thorn. She'd barely thought of him all night. 'No sign of him ever being here. Apart from that song at the harbour. Mum thinks we should just accept that he brought us here and enjoy it. Like you said.'

'And what do you think?'

'I think . . .' *What do I think?* 'I think I'm going with the flow. Drinking in the magic.'

'Mmm. You say it enough, perhaps you'll believe it, eh, chum?'

The dappled moonlight cast an unearthly glow on his coal-smudged face, creased in thought.

'I'm glad you're here, Jack,' Autumn said.

And it was nearly completely true.

24

The sun had barely risen before Jack was bouncing on her bed, insisting on being shown round the island. By the time Autumn had dragged herself from sleep and scoffed a slice of toast, Mum and The Dog had already gone next door and the house was quiet. The plum-tinted day was cold, especially with Jack lowering her temperature, so she wore one of Dad's jumpers over her dungarees.

She almost went flying over the sandbags piled up outside their own door.

'Crikey, they expecting the sea to explode or something?' Jack squinted up at the clouds, hanging over Imber like a heavy blanket. 'It's grim, but it ain't that bad.'

'It rained a lot when we first came. But it's calmed

down now.' Autumn nudged a sandbag with her foot. 'Probably just for show.'

They ambled on to the beach, kicking sand into the ocean – 'Ain't no bigger than the Thames, dunno what all the fuss is about' – and back up the coiled path on to Mordros Lane. Despite the early hour, noses poked through windows with curiosity as they walked. Autumn waved cheerfully.

'Wotcha, madam?' Jack bowed, tipping his hat and laying his cockney accent on thick. 'Roll up! Roll up! Feast your eyes on Dead Boy and Ghoul Girl: the most spectacular show on earth!'

Autumn grinned as they waved back before slinking into their homes like moles.

'They're starved of entertainment round 'ere, if *you're* the main attraction,' Jack snorted. 'No offence, chum.'

'None taken,' Autumn shot back cheerfully. 'I don't mind really, they're just curious. I saw most of them at the pub. I don't think they get Mainlanders very often.'

They wandered further than she'd been before, through an alley by The Sea Witch's Rest and down more thin steps that twisted round the cliff, ending up on the opposite side of the island. It was emptier than the harbour side, wilder – no houses, or sand, only the red-berried trees and untamed heather that spread between the rock. Autumn halted on the bottom step, the hairs on her arms standing up.

'Bit dead here, ain't it?' Jack said. 'Pardon the pun.'

It was *too* silent. Like they were the only ones left on the island. Or the world.

'C'mon.' Autumn went to turn back. 'I'm not sure we're supposed to be here. It doesn't feel right.'

'Oi.' Jack's hand went to the knife in his jacket. 'D'ya hear that?'

An eerie hum was rising from lower down the cliff, matching the rhythm of the waves. Torn between darting back to Mordros Lane and following the sound, Autumn lingered on the step, unsure.

'Better not be a ghost.' Jack backed away, holding his knife skyward. 'Curse my luck if one shows up now.'

'That's no ghost,' Autumn said, sounding more certain than she felt. 'It's not cold. So you can put the blade away.' Before she could change her mind, she leapt on to the stony ground of a cliff shelf below, halfway down the crag.

Tucked deep within the shadows were several towers of small grey stones stacked together and piled high. They stood to attention like pale soldiers.

'Well, I'll be.' Jack whistled as he popped up beside her.

Wet with sea spray, the stone towers glistened like strange opals.

'I've seen these before. Smaller ones, anyway,' Autumn said. 'Where Dad . . .' She stopped herself. 'When we were in Penzance. They're called *fairy stacks*. Tourists make them and locals hate them. None as big as these though.'

'Imber ain't a touristy sort of place, chum. So who made them?'

'I see dead people, I'm not psychic.' Autumn squinted into the darkness. 'I just want to know where that humming's coming from.'

As if she'd been summoned, an azure skirt swept into the cool sunlight, hair-jewels glinting.

'Oh, I know her!' Autumn whispered. 'She was in the pub!'

The silver-haired woman didn't notice Autumn. Her eyes were far away. She weaved between the stones until she reached the edge of the cliff, then threw her arms wide. The gentle breeze caught her scarlet shawl so that it fluttered behind her, and Autumn realized who she'd seen at the shore the other night.

'What's she doing?' Jack said. 'Learning to fly?'

Before Autumn could shush him, the woman flung her head back and began to sing a haunting melody, clear and lilting, which reached into Autumn's chest and turned her blood to sea salt.

25

'Twas many a year ago, and a day
   When a woman born of both water and fae
Did capture the heart of young Georgy of May;
They married by breaking of day, of day, they
married by breaking of day

Rest, O Fishermen, and pull up your line
The Sea Witch, she'll catch you, her older than Time.

Something about the song sent tiny pinpricks of
heat through Autumn's skin. She crept closer, so the
frayed ends of the shawl almost grazed her nose.

Their son was born in the heart of the tide,
For ten years long the woman ne'er left his side.
Till she woke to him gone, and George mournful cried,

My darling, our child has died, has died; he told her
their child had died.

Rest, O Fishermen, and pull up your line
The Sea Witch, she'll catch you, her older than Time.

The woman let her arms fall as the last note died.

'It seems my sanctuary is no longer a secret,' she said, without turning.

Autumn squeaked and stumbled backwards.

Jack chuckled. 'Ooft, somebody's in trouble,' he said, leaning against a stone tower with his hands behind his head. 'G'luck, chum.'

'I'm so sorry . . .' Autumn turned crimson. 'I didn't mean to disturb you.'

At her voice, the woman whirled round. '*Well*,' she said, tilting her head like a curious bird. She smelt of fire and ocean all at once. 'Little maid. Gone a-wandering?'

Autumn couldn't think of anything to say. Out at sea, the waves rolled and twisted, like her stomach.

'Do I scare you? Or do you greet all and sundry by gaping at them?'

'N-no,' Autumn spluttered. 'I just wondered what the humming was.'

'I see.' Gold specks sped across the woman's eyes like shooting stars. Autumn got the sense of being tested. 'Lured by music, are you?'

With the painful jar of a forgotten memory, Autumn thought of sitting on the roof of their building as Dad strummed the banjo, singing to her before bed. 'I am. I sort of grew up with it.'

'As did I,' the woman said softly.

'Sing "Daisy Bell"!' Jack yelled from the tower. Autumn shot him a withering look.

The woman gestured to the rising waves, her bracelets jangling. 'What of the sea? Or does that scare you too?'

'No,' said Autumn, almost indignantly. 'I like the sea. It feels . . . like home. But that's silly, because I've only ever lived in London – so forget I said that.'

The woman's lips rose into a wistful smile. 'Aye,' she said. 'I was named for the sea. Morvoren. The waves come and I greet them with my song. Imber is made of music and water, little maid, and I unite the two.'

'Was she one of your band lot at the pub?' asked Jack.

'Do you ever sing at the pub?' asked Autumn.

Morvoren gave a gentle scoff. '*Ha.* The music is for myself and the ocean only. Not for the jigging of fools.'

'Charming,' said Jack.

Autumn ignored him. 'That's why you were at the beach the other night. Singing to the sea.' The idea of it was weirdly tantalizing. Alone, but somehow not. 'Is it always that one about the sea witch and her child?'

'Oh, we tell more than one tale here, little maid.' Morvoren winked and gathered up her skirts. 'Keep your ears to the shore, and perhaps you'll catch one.' She swept past Autumn and ascended the thin cliff steps. 'There are as many shanties as there are stones on this island. Perhaps we'll sing one together some day.'

The sea moaned, and for one moment Autumn could imagine herself as Morvoren, calling to the shore at the dead of night.

26

'Why are you so curious, chum?' Jack leapt nimbly to his feet and followed Autumn away from the stones. 'Ain't a song just a song?'

'I don't know,' Autumn said, tucking her arms inside her jumper. The spray from the sea was making her chilly and damp. 'Dad always said that every piece of music told a story. Some of the songs they've got on Imber are sort of interesting. I'd just like to know where they come from.'

'Would've been better if she'd done "Daisy Bell".'

'All class, you.' The wind was picking up. She could feel her curls lift and tangle. 'Dad used to tell me where his songs came from. They get twisted through the years, but they always start somewhere. Like "Here We Go Round the Mulberry Bush" was about prisoners exercising in a prison yard.'

'Say, chum . . .' Jack's expression was kind, and it irritated her a bit. 'P'rhaps you're just finding it more difficult than you thought to go with the bow, that being your way. There's no ghosties here, and you like where your dad sent you. So just go with the bow.'

'Flow. It's "go with the flow".' She wished people would stop telling her that. She was doing her best. 'Let's just go home.'

There was a cold blast of air as the wind rumbled across the sea, and from somewhere beneath them there came an eerie, dull *clang* of a bell. The same one she'd heard before. Louder. Closer. Really close.

Autumn and Jack exchanged a look.

'Or maybe home can wait.'

They clambered further down the steps, winding their way towards the sea and the base of the cliff.

'I've heard that bell before,' Autumn puffed, feeling the muscles twinge at the back of her legs. 'But where's it coming from?'

Beside her, Jack flew down the steps easily. 'Well, there's your answer.'

Built within the rock – almost indistinguishable

from it – was a small, broken building with a caved-in roof and a cracked bell tower. Slate spilt on to the ground and Autumn had to concentrate to stay upright as they approached.

The bell tolled now, in sad, tinny rings. Like final breaths.

'That's a church, that is,' Jack nodded. 'It's seen better days, mind.'

Autumn stared up at the ghost of the building.

Just go with the flow, they say.

Stop worrying about everything, they say.

Maybe it was time to be brave.

'Mum won't be home for a bit. Want to take a peek?'

27

Jaw set, Autumn slipped over seaweed slime and headed for the door.

'Chum, what if it ain't safe inside?' Jack gulped. 'You could end up with your bonce bashed in. I'm engaging ghost mode.' He flitted across the stones and poked his head through the church wall, so only his soot-streaked behind was visible. He reappeared a couple of seconds later. 'It's fine, actually. Sort of ghoulish.'

'How do you mean?' Autumn wrapped her hands round the giant iron hoop handle and heaved against the door with all her might. It groaned – the wood was clearly swollen with moisture and age – and finally gave a little, leaving enough of a gap for Autumn to slip through. 'Oh, *wow*. I see what you mean.'

Pews were upturned and covered in white sludge. A cracked font was on its side, and candlesticks were broken in two. Beneath their feet was an elegant flagstone floor, names of the dead etched intricately into it. *Merryn. Finn. Tristan.* Loads of them, covered in mud and more of the white sludge. They ran towards the altar which was still draped in a dirty white cloth embroidered with the same emblem as Lamorna's cloak. It smelt like mould and melancholy.

'This is so sad,' Autumn whispered. 'It must have been beautiful in here.' Crumbs of rock scattered through the broken roof, hitting the floor like rain.

'Yeah, but is it *haunted*?' Jack lingered by the door, ready to scarper. 'Maybe all the ghosties have been hiding in here.'

'I don't think so.' It was more shades of a life lost.

As Autumn gingerly tiptoed across the flagstones, avoiding the suspect piles of goop, she pictured islanders gossiping as they crowded into church on a Sunday, singing along to shanties played on the organ which was now splintered and missing keys.

'What do you think happened?' She ran her fingers over the pillars and the walls made of crushed shells. Lying askew on the flagstones was a small book with a torn cover, *The Islander's Companion* embossed in faded silver foil on the front. It looked like one of the hymn books from Dad's funeral. 'It's like it was just abandoned.'

Jack lounged on the altar cloth like a coal-smudged god.

'Dunno. Churches were good for two things, if you ask me. Sleeping in and pickpocketing.'

Autumn threw him a disapproving glare, and he shrugged.

'Don't look at me like that. Had to supplement my living somehow.'

A faint beam of sunlight sparkled through a stained-glass window on the left wall.

'Oh, *wow*,' Autumn murmured. It was miraculously preserved. Its mosaics of blue and green showed a boy clad in robes. He stood at the shore, two gold circles at his bowed head like a halo. One inside the other. 'Who are you, then?'

With a swift hop over a broken candlestick, she climbed on to an upside-down pew. Beneath the window was a small dedication, carved with cursive lettering into a stone plaque.

Dedicated to Saint Brae, patron saint of Imber.
He heeded the call of home, but never reached its shores.

'What's that he's reaching for?' Jack asked.

Autumn peered closer. The boy's hand was outstretched, fingers splayed as if he were trying to catch something. At the far end of the window was a blur of blue and red.

'Don't know. A fish?'

'Blooming strange fish if you ask me, chum.'

A voice rang out from the doorway.

'Autumn? What are you doing in here?' Autumn swivelled and fell backwards on to the flagstones in a heap.

28

'Oh goodness, are you hurt?' Lamorna Hawthorn swam into view, upside down. She was flanked by two glossy red setters.

Winded, embarrassed and possibly with – yep, there it was – white sludge in her hair, Autumn scrambled to her feet and grinned absurdly.

'Absotootly fine! Lamorna! Lovely to see you! Just passing, or . . . ?'

'So this is Lamorna, eh?' Jack dived off the altar and floated towards the sad-eyed girl, eyeing her wide smile and perfect teeth, her expensive clothes. 'Smells funny. Flowery.'

Lamorna picked a piece of seaweed from Autumn's coat. 'I often come and sit in here. Sometimes alone. Sometimes with Neptune and Triton.'

The two dogs sat rigidly on either side of her, as elegant and still as stone angels. If they'd noticed the ghost pulling faces at them, they'd been well trained enough not to bark. 'I'm surprised to see you on this part of the island. There's nothing of interest here, but it calms me, doesn't it, boys?' She rubbed the dogs' silky ears. 'Are you sure you're quite well?'

'Tip-top,' Autumn said, feeling like she'd been caught doing something wrong. 'I just wondered what this was.'

'St Brae's. It was the fisherman's chapel,' Lamorna said. 'The oldest thing on Imber. My ancestors built it, I believe, but alas, it did not survive the flood.'

'The flood?' Autumn glanced at Jack. 'How many floods have there been?'

'Get out, Autumn, get out now.' Jack was already at the door, bobbing on his heels. 'I remember the Thames flooding in '28. It weren't good.'

Lamorna sidestepped a pile of rocks. 'Oh, just the one. The fact the church lasted for centuries this close to sea level is tribute to the flood's . . . abnormality.'

Autumn's wrinkled forehead must have given her away.

'Honestly, there's no need for concern, Autumn. I promise you,' Lamorna said. 'My family have ensured that . . .' She paused, looking momentarily flustered. 'I mean to say, it won't happen again.' It might have been her imagination, but Autumn could have sworn Lamorna paled, her eyes flicking to the altar. But it didn't last. A trick of the light.

'Well, we've left it like this so nobody forgets,' Lamorna continued brightly. 'We keep the island safe. Always.'

'Sandbags ain't *that* good,' muttered Jack.

'Stop panicking,' Autumn whispered as she followed Lamorna back outside. 'We're Mainlanders remember? What do we know?' The morning's grey light made her eyes blurry after the gloom of the church.

'Now, I have a proposition for you.' Lamorna placed a white palm on each setter's head. They nuzzled into her hands. 'Would you like to visit my home tomorrow? Say, when the sun is highest?'

'What's wrong with saying noon?' grunted Jack, loitering as far away as he could without being *pinged* back into the playing card.

The blood was shooting round Autumn's ears like

gunfire. She'd been invited to someone's house. *Her*. *She*, who had been left out of every party invitation, every sleepover, every popcorn-and-movie night. The spare part. The weirdo.

She wanted to wrap Lamorna in a bear hug. Instead, she murmured, 'Thank you much' and burnt scarlet.

'Marvellous!' Lamorna seemed just as thrilled as Autumn. 'You'll find it at Imber's highest point. Follow the main island road as far as it will go. Oh – and it's not as big as they say.' With a wave, she climbed the steps effortlessly, the dogs following her tread like rusty shadows.

'Only toffs say stuff like that,' Jack grumbled. 'Bet the house is gigantic.'

'Honey, I'm going back to Fred and Beth's. I said I'd pop over with some exercises.' Mum scampered back and forth, running circles round Autumn who was sucking on an orange and thinking about all the stupid things she'd ever said.

'Exercises?'

'For his dementia. Just a few puzzles to keep his mind ticking over. It'll be nice to use my brain for once. It's turned to mush since I stopped working at the care home.'

She rifled through her old work bag, and Autumn realized just how long it had been since she saw Mum this focused.

'Can I come?' She was suddenly desperate to switch her own brain off, even just for an evening. Jack had retired to the chimney, quiet and grumpy and homesick for the smell of fire. 'I won't get in the way.'

Mum's face lit up with her giant, infectious smile. Dad had loved that smile. He said it was like the first ray of sunshine after a rainstorm.

'Yeah, I mean, why wouldn't you want to hang out? Look at me, I'm aces.'

'Well don't ruin it, Mum.'

Mum pushed her tortoiseshell glasses up her nose. 'I'll be super cool, don't worry. I'm sure Fred'll be happy to see you. He's got a soft spot for you, you know.'

29

Wet clothes hung near the Emlyns' fire. Fred's hair was tousled and damp, his cheeks reddened with seawater and cold air. He grinned widely as Autumn sat next to him at the table.

'Nippy at dusk, isn't it little one?' he said. 'Lovely weather for a dip.'

'You what now?' Mum said, warming her fingers by the fire. 'It's the depths of winter.' She was bulky in two jumpers. Beth had insisted they stay for dinner and the kitchen's steaming warmth made Autumn dozily calm.

Bracken had even settled at her feet, snuggled up with The Dog.

'He went out swimming, if you can believe it.' Beth pottered at the stove, clanging baking trays and saucepans. A delicious smell filled the kitchen. 'The worse the weather is, the more this man longs for the sea.'

Autumn looked up at Fred beside her – the bright eyes, the strong arms. He looked younger today. As if the water had cast a spell.

Fred guffawed. 'Ah, there's nothing like a stormy-sea swim. If you can swim in a storm, you can swim anywhere. Got to keep strong, haven't I, Elizabeth?'

'If you say so, my dear.' Beth sounded weary. She slipped flowery oven gloves over her hands and plonked a half-moon-shaped pastry on Autumn's plate. It was crimped round the edge. 'It's a vegan Cornish pasty,' she said proudly. 'It took five attempts, but I did it.'

Autumn took a grateful bite. The pasty warmed her insides.

'And how are you finding Imber, Autumn? Not quite what you're used to, I bet?'

'It's different, Mrs Emlyn,' she said through a mouthful of potatoes and gravy. 'But I like the trad-itions. And the songs.'

Fred roared with laughter, his blue eyes flashing. 'If you say so, little one. All our myths and legends can scare some Mainlanders off. Just ask this emmet here.' He gestured to his wife. 'Elizabeth, you got a fright when you came to this island, didn't you?'

Autumn looked up in surprise. 'Oh, I thought you were born here.'

'Not a chance,' Beth chuckled. 'I'm from Bristol. I was charmed enough by this one on a visit to Cornwall,' she nodded at Fred, 'to leave everything I knew and move to this godforsaken place.'

'I know a little about that,' mumbled Mum, keeping her eyes low. 'How did you guys meet?'

There was a whimper, and Fred dropped his pasty on to his plate. 'I have to get to Sennen Cove, Miss Elizabeth,' he said quietly, staring at nothing. 'My boat's there and the flood's a-coming. Have to get home.' Bracken jumped on to his lap and tucked her head under his chin, unnoticed.

Beth froze mid-mouthful. The only sound came from the ticking of the clock on the dresser. Autumn wanted to say something to make Fred all right again, but she felt awkward and clumsy and didn't want to make anything worse.

Mum wiped her mouth with her napkin and laid her hand gently on Fred's shoulder. 'Hey, Fred –

eight down, do you remember?'

Fred's gaze cleared, and suddenly he was back in the room again. 'Remember it?' He turned to Beth and Autumn, the lines of his face cracking into a smile. 'Madam here tried to put *Picasso*.' He patted Mum on the back with a big hand. 'Any fool knows the Water-Lilies was *Monet*. Good job I like you, Sarah, else we'd be finding new neighbours.'

Autumn watched her mum come alive, feeling both incredibly proud and incredibly useless. Mum was so good with talking. And with people. She'd never been like that. She was like Dad. A bit strange.

Sometimes, my love, alone is the safest place.

'Any adventures for you this weekend, Autumn?' Beth asked, before finally biting into her own pasty.

'I think so, Mrs Emlyn. I'm meeting Lamorna tomorrow, at her house.'

The Emlyns exchanged a brief look, eyebrows raised.

'Well!' chuckled Beth. 'Mixing up at the Big House, eh? You'll be too good for the likes of us soon.'

'Ha ha ha.' Autumn gave a wobbly laugh.

'You know, there are some other lovely youngsters

on the island too . . .' Beth chattered through her pasty. 'Caja Pendragon, Johnny Boatswain . . .'

Autumn smiled absently and tried to ignore the fear that burnt when she thought about visiting Lamorna.

What if she said something stupid? What if Lamorna realized she was weird and didn't want to be friends any more?

Just how was she going to mess this one up?

30

'See? Told you,' Jack said triumphantly. 'Huge.'

They'd followed the track as far as it would go, winding to the top of the island. To the snake's mouth.

From lower down, the dark hulk of Imber's peak had seemed to be only the tip of the cliffs, but up-close Autumn saw a stately building built into them, soaked in shadow. A flag whipped from a pointed turret; two gold circles, one inside the other.

'It's not *that* massive,' Autumn said, her teeth chattering. It was. There must have been about twenty windows. 'Remember the condition of you coming along? You stop moaning about Lamorna. What do you have against her, anyway?'

Jack scratched his mop of hair and ash flew,

swiftly snatched by the wind. 'She's just rich, ain't she? Never had much time for them that hoard money – not with some of the stuff I've seen.' He turned his cap over in his hands before plonking it back on his head. 'But if you say she's all right, chum, then she's all right. I'll stop griping.'

Ahead stood ornately carved gates with 'Hawthorn' cast in iron. With a deep breath, Autumn heaved them open and edged into a court-yard bordered with red-berried trees. A large fountain was in the centre, a mermaid pouring water from a conch shell.

'Autumn!' Angelic in cream cashmere, Lamorna appeared at the doorway and waved her inside. 'Do come in – the wind is *wild* today. You must be frozen through!'

The Dog yanked her back, plonking himself behind Jack's legs.

'He ain't a fan either, Autumn,' Jack sniggered.

'Is it OK I brought him?' Autumn suddenly wondered if it was rude to bring your pet to some-body else's house. 'My mum's with our neighbours and he gets a bit nervous there.' She didn't add *because a ghost beagle keeps baiting him.*

'Absolutely!' The Dog farted anxiously, and Lamorna cooed as if he'd done something adorable. 'Perhaps he'd like to spend time with my pets? Neptune and Triton you've met, and there's Zennor the horse, too. She has a brother, Rowan, and there are also our cats and the birds. We have a whole wing for the animals.'

'Of course they blooming do,' Jack scoffed. At Autumn's glare he cowered in mock contrition. 'All right, all right. I'll behave. Ever so 'umble, that's me.'

Lamorna ushered them inside and Autumn found herself standing on a pristine marble floor, chequered black and white like a chessboard. The entrance hall resembled a museum, hushed and arched and old – all wood and portraits and musty smell. She was suddenly keenly aware of her wild hair frizzed with damp air, and her boots scuffing the floor. She must have looked a right state.

With a worried whimper, The Dog was shepherded off by a silent man in suit tails, his shaggy tail brushing the floor like a broom. Autumn blew him a kiss.

'Bye, mutt,' Jack called. 'Whatever you do, don't

wee on their carpet.'

The Dog yelped sharply in response. Lamorna paused and followed his gaze to the dead chimney sweep, frozen mid-step. 'That's odd, Autumn,' she said curiously. 'He's barking at an empty corner of the room. Does he often do that?'

The familiar buzzing started in Autumn's head.

'Oh, er . . . he's just . . . he's just high maintenance. That's all. Has a lot of feelings, you know.'

Lamorna nodded in sympathy. 'Oh well, that I understand. He'll have a marvellous time with the setters, don't worry.'

'Say *nothing*, Jack,' Autumn whispered under her breath as Lamorna beckoned them up an oak staircase. 'I mean it.'

'As if I would.' He skipped up beside her, his heavy boots noiseless on the wooden steps. 'Cor, look at all them portraits. Serious-looking lot, those Hawthorns, weren't they?'

There they were, lining the panelled walls as they ascended, all disapproving with grey eyes burning into her as she passed. *Lord Uther, Lady Ariadne, Lord Branok, Lady Isolde . . .*

'Miss Albert!'

Jiggling with excitement on the landing was the current lord of the manor, merrier than all his ancestors put together.

31

Lord Hawthorn wore a silk waistcoat decorated with peacock feathers, a green velvet cap and mismatched slippers. Crumbs of bread were trapped in his beard.

'Lord Hawthorn, sir,' Autumn mumbled.

Jack halted beside her. 'It's Father blooming Christmas.'

Frantic hands waved them up. 'Come, come, come!' His face shone under the chandelier's light. 'Such a pleasure to see you, my dear. I hope the cold air did not trouble you too much. Or are you truly an Imberian now, and impervious to it?'

'Oh, I don't mind!' She'd got words out in the right order, that was something. Even if her voice was weirdly high. 'At least it hasn't rained for a while.'

This appeared to be the correct answer. He giggled and his cheeks grew pinker.

'Quite right, quite right; it has not! Let us hope this is not the calm before the storm, eh?'

With a final *boom* of a hand clap, he bounded towards another room, flickering with firelight. 'I offer ardent apologies for my absence, Miss Albert. As Imber's custodian, duty is never-ending. I must keep this island safe, my dear, always.' He twirled on his heels. 'Oh, tush. Lamorna? I'm a silly, absent-minded fool.'

His daughter rolled her eyes. '*What*, father?'

'I meant to ask, how is your little task going? Any luck identifying our new seabird?'

'The seabird is in hand,' Lamorna replied through gritted teeth. 'It will be identified soon. Now leave me and Autumn *be*, will you?'

'But of course, darling girl.' He toddled off like a happy toad. 'Delightful to see you again, Miss Albert. Do help yourself to the truffles in the hallway.'

'*I must keep this island safe, always!*' Jack parroted in his best imitation. Autumn stuffed a hand in her mouth to keep from giggling. 'And what was all that about a seabird? This lot ain't half peculiar.'

'I'm terribly sorry about him.' Lamorna gave herself a shake and her composure settled back on her like a winter coat. 'Hawthorns always give their first-born certain tasks, like dropping crumbs from a plate. Father believes it will help me learn my future role. Of course, I have it in hand.'

She tutted and they shuffled into a large oval room, mahogany and thick with the smell of old paper.

'Blooming heck,' said Jack.

'Oh, *cripes*.' Autumn inhaled. 'You have your own library?'

The walls, dark red and decked with candlesticks, boasted acres of hardback books lined up on laddered shelves. Taxidermic sea creatures glared at her from corners and faded tapestries hung from walls. Above a neat desk hung a large – and frankly flattering – portrait of Lord Hawthorn; one hand on a jacked-up horse, the other grasping a white flower.

Lamorna sank into a velvet chaise longue in the middle of the room. 'Do help yourself to whatever you wish. Each book contains a veritable plethora of Imber facts. Our family traditionally allowed the islanders in once a month to educate them.'

'Oh, for . . .' Clamping his mouth shut, Jack turned his back on them both and hopped on to the mantelpiece. 'Keeping quiet.'

Autumn scanned the titles hungrily – *Chucky-Pigs: A Much-Maligned Species*, *Spells of the Sea: Summon, Banish and Bewitch*, *Tides and the Moon* and *The Hawthorn Dynasty* – before her eyes settled on one and her heart leapt.

'Can I take this one, please? *The Islander's Companion*?' It was the same book she'd seen in the church. It felt important, somehow, that someone read it again.

'Whatever you wish,' Lamorna replied, distracted. 'Now, I wonder . . .' She straightened and ran delicate fingers over the book spines, her expression thoughtful. 'I have a fancy for doing something different today.'

'OK,' said Autumn, slipping the small book into her dungarees pocket.

'Well, this'll be interesting.' Jack stretched laconically on the mantelpiece. 'Throwing coins at peasants?'

Autumn shot daggers at him and allowed herself to be led to a large sash window overlooking the beach. The sea was angrier than she'd ever seen it, rearing like a horse on its hind legs and smashing down on to the crag.

'You haven't been in yet, have you?' Lamorna mused, tracing two circles in the window mist.

'In?'

'Into the sea. Swimming.'

32

Understanding struck her like lightning.

'Er, no. No, I haven't.'

Jack must have clocked at the same time because he leapt off the mantelpiece and flew to the window. 'What is she thinking? Nobody could swim that and survive. And chum, you can't swim at all.'

Autumn cringed. What with Dad's fear and Mum never wanting her at the local pool because of verrucas and wee, she'd just never got round to it. Right then she'd have cut off her nose to go back in time and learn how to doggy-paddle.

'You don't know the meaning of thrill until you've swum in an Imber wind, Autumn. It's magical.' Lamorna clasped Autumn's hands in hers. They were icy cold and pocked with goosebumps. 'Do you see that?'

Autumn followed Lamorna's finger. She was pointing at the stone arch, protruding from the waves.

'Just about.'

'That's Brae's Rock. Legend has it only a *true* Imberian can reach it. What do you say we test the theory today?'

It looked pretty far away, Brae's Rock.

Before Autumn could formulate the words to protest, she was pulled through a door in the wall and down a different staircase which spiralled round and round towards the bowels of the house.

A blur of brick, and they were in a room, marine-blue and small. Aside from the wall, which was adorned with sea glass and a mural of a mermaid and three starfish, it seemed empty.

'Lamorna.' Autumn found her voice just as Jack *swooshed* in, wound up like a coiled spring. 'I don't have a swimming costume. And I can't . . . that is, I've never . . .'

Don't tell her you can't swim. She'll laugh you off the island.

'Fret not, Autumn. I have something ready, for

just such an occasion.'

Oh, good.

Flushed with excitement, Lamorna pressed the tip of her finger to a shard of amber sea glass. There was a shuffle and a groan of hinges, and a door swung slowly from the mermaid's tail.

'Secret doors!' Lamorna laughed, seeing her face. 'This is only a cupboard, but the Sea Glass Room is a gateway. Secret doors are everywhere. You'd *never* suspect where they are. Much of the sea glass is just sea glass.'

'You can't actually be thinking of doing this Autumn, surely?' Jack was at her shoulder, his anger spreading frosty patterns at her feet.

'I . . .' she began, not sure who she was talking to.

'Slip this on and I'll meet you outside in a moment.' Lamorna gave her an encouraging smile, lightly touching a piece of brown sea glass before vanishing through another imperceptible door.

'Chum, don't do this, not after your da.' Jack stared at her earnestly, turning his cap round his hands. 'We'll go home and we'll listen to your ma's records and you'll eat sandwiches and we'll pretend like this never happened, wotcha say?'

'Jack, I'm not going to do it. Just give me a minute to think of an excuse.' She squeezed the wetsuit over her dungarees like an overstuffed ham. Was she supposed to take her clothes off first? *Oh, well, too late.* And what was a good excuse? What could she say that would make Lamorna not despise her, or think she was a coward?

Her brain still spinning, she tapped the sea glass and followed Lamorna through the secret door.

33

She came out in the heart of a cave, black and icy cold.

'Follow my voice!' Lamorna shouted from the beach, almost muffled by the wind. 'Head towards the mouth of the cave.'

Autumn faltered on wet stone, her feet sliding into rock pools. A deep pool of seawater snaked alongside her and out into the ocean, so she followed it until she reached the open air at the cave's entrance. Her skin was smacked by the wind's blast.

The faint clang of the church bell came in short, sharp cries.

'Welcome, friend!' Lamorna stood astride a pile of rocks. She held out her hand and helped Autumn clamber across and down on to the sand. Autumn had already managed to get herself soaked in seaweed and dirt.

Why does Lamorna look like a model in her wetsuit and I look like a squashed tree?

'Isn't it glorious?'

Autumn's ears were so full, it was hard to make out what Lamorna was saying.

How do you swim anyway? she thought frantically. *Kick legs and feet at the same time? One at a time? Two at a time?*

'Of course, I wouldn't force you to do anything, Autumn, anything at all.' Shaking in the wind, Lamorna looked almost as transparent as a ghost. 'But you're my friend and I want to share something wonderful with you. You'd be safe the whole time. I'm the best swimmer on the island.'

It was hard to believe. Lamorna looked as delicate as paper. *But then again,* Autumn thought in surprise, feeling the waves smack against the rocks, *I don't think I'm actually scared.*

And she wasn't. Despite Dad drowning, despite the violence of the ocean and the force of the wind, she was kind of desperate to dive in. It was calling her like the voice of a sea siren.

And Lamorna looked so hopeful. If she refused now, that would be *it* for their friendship.

I have to do it.

'Autumn.' Jack was by her side suddenly, his voice low, his eyes dark. 'You don't have to do this. You don't need to prove nothing to nobody.'

She unzipped her wetsuit and slipped a hand into her pocket, pulled out its contents and hid them in a dip in the rock underneath some seaweed.

'Stay here, near your card,' she whispered. 'It's OK. If a ninety-year-old man can swim in a storm, then so can I. I've got this.'

'No, you blooming haven't . . . *Autumn*!'

Without letting herself think, she bounded across the sand with Lamorna behind her, beaming with joy.

'Do it, Autumn!' she cried. 'Dive in!'

And then her legs were in the ocean and she was breathless with the shock of it, dimly aware of Jack screaming her name.

I'm going with the flow.

34

She closed her eyes, held her nose and belly-flopped on to the waves. They lurched her back and forth like flotsam, with her head in and out of the ocean just long enough to catch gasping breaths and a mouthful of sea foam. Tangled curls – or was it seaweed? – stuck to her eyelids, her mouth, snaking up her nostrils.

Maybe swimming was harder than it looked.

Another plunge beneath the waves. The surface wibbled above her head like smoke. She reached towards it.

A blurred shadow darkened the water.

Lamorna?

Autumn felt a hand slip into hers and she ceased her kicking as she was pulled to the top. She broke through and allowed herself to float with the weight of the ocean beneath her back.

Lamorna was nowhere to be seen. She was the only one there.

'You're all right?' Jack's call was strangled. 'Tell me you're all right!'

'I'm all right!' she managed, though it felt like she'd swallowed a chainsaw. Instinctively she flipped over, twisting her arms and legs like a paddle. She crawled forward, on and on, carried by the tide until she was sweeping through the waves as if they were silk.

I'm doing it. I'm actually swimming!

'You wonder!' Lamorna's joyful call was far behind her.

'Chum, she's left you out there alone!' Jack shouted.

Autumn barely heard him. With each stroke she grew stronger until the sea seemed to bend to her will, the fierce swell of the waves calming at her touch. Brae's Rock was drawing nearer and with a swanlike ease that she'd *never* possessed on land, her whole body spun through the water like a mermaid.

At last, the archway was in touching distance. She

reached out with trembling arms and her legs bumped something beneath the surface. Gripping on to the rock, she dipped her head underwater and peered into the grey murk.

It wasn't an archway at all. It was a huge, circular stone with a hole worn through the middle. A giant version of Dad's.

Limbs woolly, she hoisted herself up on it, barely registering the painful scrape of barnacles or the bruise of skin upon stone. She sat in the centre of the circle like a queen on her throne, and electricity prickled at her skin.

'Lamorna!' Autumn screamed, throwing her arms into the air. 'I made it!'

Lamorna's answering *whoop* was like medicine. Autumn had never been proud of herself, not ever – she'd never done anything worth celebrating – but this felt like winning a gold medal at the Olympics. She threw her head back and tasted the air. The electric feeling grew stronger, burning her legs and her arms.

'Chum, hoorah and everything, but *please* come back now.' She could see Jack straining forward, desperate to remove himself from the card's grasp.

'Let's go home, eh?'

'Oh, fine.' Reluctantly she wiggled her bottom closer to the edge, ready to lower herself into the sea. The electricity sparked her legs like burning needles.

Find me.

A voice came from nowhere. She couldn't make out who it belonged to, whether old or young, male or female.

Find me.

It was like a scratch against a chalkboard.

The voice came again, right behind her.

Find me!

Autumn whirled round. There was someone there. She could feel the change in the atmosphere – that cold, familiar tingle at the back of her neck. A ghost.

Find me!

The blurry shadow from the sea crackled to life like sheet lightning. Her stomach tightened with something. It felt like longing. Yearning for home.

'Who are you?' she whispered. 'I can't see your face.'

Find me!

As if someone had pulled a plug, it vanished, and a burst of electricity scalded her. She fell backwards into the sea with a hard *splash*.

'Autumn!' came Lamorna's screech from far away. 'Where are you?'

'Down here!' she cried, or she would have done if she could speak. Instead, she swallowed mouthfuls of saltwater and her lungs burnt.

She couldn't see Lamorna. She couldn't see Jack. She couldn't even see the beach any more.

I shouldn't have done this, came the sudden, panicked thought. *I shouldn't have done this*.

Daylight faded into blue mist as she kicked wildly, trying to find the seafloor, but there was nothing beneath her feet, only more sea, and the sinking feeling that she was going to die the same way as Dad, choking and floundering and reaching for air that would never come.

'Alley-oop, dear girl.' A friendly call and Lord Hawthorn was pulling her out of the ocean and plonking her into his sailboat. She spat out the sea and lay on her back as they rode over the waves like a rollercoaster. 'You did absolutely splendidly.' His voice was a muffled cheer over the roar in her ears.

'Only a true Imberian can get to Brae's Rock, you know. You really are one of us.'

That thought kept her warm as they reached the shore.

I'm one of them. I belong.

35

'Why did you do that?' Jack demanded, looking as close to tears as she'd ever seen him. 'You could have been killed, Autumn . . . *dead*. And that ain't nice, believe me.'

Heart pounding out of her chest, she sank on to the sand. It was like she was breathing air for the first time. She smiled.

'Autumn!' Lamorna ran across the beach and flung herself at her feet. 'You're spectacular! You did it! Only the most accomplished ever reach Brae's Rock without turning back.'

'Exactly.' Jack knelt beside her, and the mingled smell of smoke and seawater made her dizzy. ''Cept you ain't never swum before. So what's that all about then?'

*

That night, Autumn tucked herself up in bed with a raspberry tea and *The Islander's Companion*. She'd left her curtains open so she could watch the sunset but now it was pitch black. Despite a long bath, every part of her ached and her curls were still crunchy with salt. She liked it.

She hadn't told Mum about everything that had happened. It felt like her own delicious secret.

'It's all barmy.' Jack paced the small room, babbling in cockney. 'What was that gigglemug Lamorna *thinking*? And when did you suddenly turn into a salmon?'

Autumn opened her mouth. She knew what she should say. *There was a voice, Jack. A hand. Someone was there.* She shut it again. If it had been anything, it was long gone.

'Everyone can swim. I didn't do anything special. And Lamorna's a good person,' Autumn mumbled. 'She's my friend.'

'*I'm* your friend,' Jack muttered grumpily, fading into the fireplace. 'But I don't have bones, do I, so I don't matter.'

Too tired to argue, Autumn bit her tongue and

146

focused her eyes on the book, a pale yellow in the lamplight. As well as the lyrics for the church's shanties – she spotted Morvoren's 'Rest, O Fisherman' and some of the tunes from the pub – it was a sort of bible for everything Imber. Poems, maps, recipes for samphire tea and seaweed bread, pictures of the islanders going about their daily lives.

The idea of the book being washed away gave her the shivers. And St Brae's being ripped apart by the strength of the sea. How long had it been sitting in the rock, frozen in time? How long since the flood came?

She skimmed through, looking at old photographs of smocked fishermen down by the harbour, a group of young girls climbing a red-berried tree. A young man stood proudly holding a large vegetable – *GW and his prize-winning marrow, 1954*, according to the caption – and two freckled children (*W&L, 1937*) smiled by the sea, collecting shells in a basket.

'Honey, lights out soon, OK?' Mum popped her head round the door, The Dog snuffling at her feet. 'You look exhausted. Get some rest.'

'Will do. Night, Mum.'

She flipped the page, and her blood turned to ice.

No.

Halfway down the page was a black-and-white picture of a serious-looking boy – probably a bit older than her – sitting on the harbour wall with his legs crossed. He was looking beyond the photographer and out to sea, his broad arms propping him up. He wore his shirt sleeves rolled to the elbow.

The caption below read *LT, 1989.*

'Jack?' Autumn called in a hoarse whisper, the thudding of her heart feeling louder than her voice. 'You need to see this.'

The young man in the picture was beardless, there were no crow's feet at the edges of his eyes, but it was unmistakeably him.

Dad.

36

Jack looked even more rumpled than usual.

Autumn skipped from one leg to the other and shoved the picture under his nose. 'Jack, *look*! It's Dad, I know it. It's the same face, it's him, he would've been fourteen here, so it matches up, don't you think? Can you *believe* it?'

The Dog bounded through the door and pressed his nose on to the paper with an excited whine. Autumn hadn't heard that whine since Dad's study.

It was so strange, seeing him at her own age. He had her cleft chin, the same freckle under his eye.

'Cor,' Jack whistled. 'That's him, no doubt. Doesn't look chirpy, though. Why'd he never talk about Imber?'

'I have no idea. Mum said he'd always been

mysterious. He must have been hiding from some-thing. Maybe his mum and dad? I never knew them.'

'Go and show it to your ma! She'll be cock-a-hoop!'

'Um . . .' What with the ghosts, Autumn had got used to keeping things from Mum. And she'd been doing so well here, making friends with the Emlyns. 'I don't want to drag her back down by reminding her of Dad and his secrets. She's focusing on new stuff now.'

'Fair dos. Well, just go and show this picture to Lamorna or your neighbours and then perhaps we'll learn more about him!'

The idea sat like lead in her stomach. Yes, there was Beth's warning about keeping quiet – and she knew from the stares that the islanders loved a bit of gossip – but it didn't seem fair to expose the past Dad had tried to keep hidden. Not to strangers, anyway.

And there was the other tiny, scratchy panic. What if they discovered something about him that could upset everything? What if it made Lamorna stop liking her?

Yep. The more of him, and her, she kept hidden, the better.

'No. I don't want to ask anybody on Imber,' she said. An idea was bubbling. 'But I know exactly who I *can* ask . . .'

Two days later, Autumn sat on the harbour jetty with the wind whipping her hair into straw and wondered how often Dad had sat there too.

Another huge wave roared and pounded into the stone. She stayed put. The sea held no fear for her, not now, and Lamorna had promised the Hawthorns would protect them from another flood. Watching the titan strength of the ocean, Autumn couldn't help but wonder how.

Who had Dad been? Was he happy on Imber, before whatever-it-was sent him packing, never to return? Had his love of music started here? Was his love of birds inspired by the cormorants diving and sandpipers probing for insects?

She longed to know what he'd been hiding. If she knew what it was, she'd feel closer to him somehow.

'All well, little one?'

With a start, Autumn saw Fred appear at the end of the jetty. He was in boots and overalls, soaked to the shins.

'Where did you come from, Fred? The rock pools?'

'It's not just rock pools I'm searching. Could be anywhere. The caves. The maythorns.'

'Maythorns?'

'Hawthorn trees. Some call 'em maythorns. Red berries.'

Fred peered off the jetty to where he'd come from. 'Not in the boat.' With that, a hand was thrown up in farewell and Fred was away, muttering as he disappeared up the track.

At last, a horn moaned and the Imber ferry battled with the waves, barely reaching the slipway without being pulled under. It was back, finally. It seemed the island wasn't worth visiting more than once a week.

Wrong to its bones.

Autumn ran to the end of the jetty just in time to see the ferry ramp lower sluggishly, the sea pouring from it like a waterfall. Nobody got off. Nobody got on. At the controls, the skipper frowned and grumbled something into a radio.

The pale ferryman stood on the deck, alone and perfectly dry.

'Ahoy there!' Autumn called up, and his glassy

eyes turned on her. She shivered with the ghostly temperature shift.

'You,' he said.

Her stomach churned, but she stood firm. 'Can you help me? I need to know about a passenger you might have had.' She held up the book page, already wet with the surf. 'Do you recognize him? Did you ever give him a ride away from here?'

The ferryman glared at her, and her insides turned cold.

'There's a local legend round here, y'know. This island is wrong to its bones. Any true Cornishman stays away.'

'I know. You've said that.' Autumn's impatience rose. 'But did you see him? Please?'

The boat's engine spluttered to life.

'No.'

Autumn's heart sank like cement. 'Right. Thanks.'

Spitting seawater, the boat began to turn. The ferryman stayed unmoving on the deck, but his voice sounded in her ear as clearly as if he were behind her.

'Round the West, most legends start with a stone.'

'A stone?' Autumn leant as far off the jetty as she

could without falling in. 'What do you mean? What do you know?'

'Not for me to say.' The boat chugged closer to the mainland, leaving Autumn a solitary figure at the harbour. 'Not for me to say.'

37

'Now there's a face I know.' There were steady footsteps on the jetty. Morvoren sidled next to Autumn.

In the early afternoon light, her hair seemed greyer somehow, the lines of her face darker and more pronounced. 'You've something on your mind, little maid. Tell a friend your tale?'

Autumn slipped the book back into her coat and hesitated before answering. 'Odd question, but . . . someone told me that a lot of legends in the West start with stones. Is there something special about them?' Saying it out loud made it sound daft.

Far from laughing her into the sea, Morvoren seemed to consider this for a moment. 'Aye. Perhaps. Some say. The West is soaked with henges, monoliths, stone circles. Kings drawing swords. Saints throwing rocks at giants. Stones have been here since the dawn of time: more ancient than all of us.' She winced as she cracked her neck, half-smiling. 'Well, some of us.'

'So do people think they're magic or something?'

'Well, little maid, what do you think?'

A strange feeling was growing in Autumn's belly, like the rising of a wave or the burst of a storm cloud.

Dad's stone. His picture. The crackling, shadowy ghost from Brae's Rock. *Find me.*

Had that been him?

Maybe the stone *wasn't* Dad's talisman. But she had the strongest feeling that none of this was a coincidence. Who was to say a stone couldn't still bring his ghost back?

Were *these* the breadcrumbs she was always meant to follow?

'Thank you, Morvoren,' she gabbled, jumping to her feet before the inspiration deserted her. 'You've been really helpful.'

The singer rose gracefully and drew her shawl against the wind. 'There's a first time for everything. And . . . little maid?'

'Yes?'

The two of them swapped gazes.

'Whatever is troubling you,' Morvoren whispered, 'remember that a single wave does not make an ocean. Do you understand?'

'I . . . I do.' She didn't, but Morvoren's face made her stomach clench. It had changed. Pain etched her skin.

'Ah, little maid,' Morvoren murmured, as another giant wave hammered the jetty. 'It means you are not alone. But sometimes, alone is the safest place.'

Autumn watched her go; an old woman huddled into her shawl, fighting against the wind.

Autumn darted up the coiled path until she landed at the Hawthorn House gates. She hoisted them open and ran to the porch, yanking the bell chain with blue hands.

'Autumn! What are you doing here?' Lamorna appeared behind the door, looking pale-faced and tired and wrapped in a silk dressing gown. An orange cat curled itself around her knees. 'Do you wish to come and sit by the fire?'

The wooden warmth of the entrance hall was rather tempting. She could feel the fire's heat from outside.

'Thank you, no.' Autumn reached into her bag and pulled out *The Islander's Companion*. 'I've been enjoying this. I wanted to bring it back. Is it OK if I borrow another one?'

'Goodness, you are the voracious reader, aren't you?' Lamorna said. 'Would you mind putting it back exactly where you got it? Despite the ragtag veneer, Father's a stickler for order. Although he barely reads. He just wishes to *look* intelligent.' She laughed bitterly. 'You remember where the library is?'

'Thank you,' Autumn yelled back as she bounded up the stairs two at a time. She scurried into the red-walled room, ran to the bookshelf and brushed her fingers along the spines until she found the one she remembered.

'Got one!' She waved it in the air cheerfully as she descended the stairs to the entrance hall. 'Got to go before Mum gets home.'

'I see.' Lamorna sounded sad as she lingered by the door. 'May we meet tomorrow? Say, by the harbour at mid-morning? I so enjoyed our sojourn.'

'Of course!' Autumn wheeled round and the violet-eyed girl beamed happily. 'Me too!'

She crossed the courtyard with a spring in her

step. As the iron gates swung shut behind her, she paused and held the book to her chest. Hardbacked and ebony-coloured. The promise of a new hope.

Spells of the Sea: Summon, Banish and Bewitch.

38

Sprinkle crushed sea holly on to lit
charcoals, or in a flaming cauldron.
Place the deceased's object in the
heart of the fire.
Legend has it that they will
emerge from the flame.

She'd flipped through until she finally found it nestled between 'A Spell to Enliven a Seal' and 'A Charm to Induce Nightmares', gobbling up every incantation and charm along the way. Iron repels witchcraft and magic. Hemlock solves discord. Blackberry root protects.

As for sea holly, it seemed the coast was riddled with it. She grabbed as much of the blue, thistle-like flower as she could without it looking suspicious.

All through dinner she stared at the clock, willing it to speed up so Mum would go to bed. Jack seemed even more nervous than she was; he was chattering nineteen to the dozen about the sports he'd watched on Mr Mazur's television.

'. . . Course, there was Euro '96, that was a heart-stopper I'll tell you, but that was years before you were born weren't it – but penalties are tough, I wouldn't want to do it. Mind, football wouldn't be my game at all, on account of stubby legs. Nah, I'd have been a jockey I reckon.'

Autumn breathed in time with the tide and tried to keep calm.

'I've got some news,' announced Mum, as they washed up the plates. 'I've got a job.'

Autumn tore her eyes from the clock's second hand, which seemed to be going backwards. 'What? Mum, that's brilliant. Where?'

'Next door. I'm going to be Fred's official carer. His condition's getting worse and Beth needs profes-sional help. So, from tomorrow, if I'm not here, I'm there.'

'That's both sad and good. Well done, Mum. I'm

so proud of you.' Suddenly overcome, Autumn surprised herself by leaning on Mum's shoulder.

Mum kissed her forehead. 'Wow, voluntary physical affection and everything? You doing OK?!'

Autumn thought about Dad's photograph and his stone and the possibility of everything, and came so close to spilling her guts that she had to clamp her mouth shut. *Don't get her hopes up.*

Instead, she snuggled in and said in a small voice, 'I'm good, Mum. I'm really good.'

Mum took herself to bed at ten o'clock, carrying a snoring Dog in his blanket. Autumn and Jack waited outside her door for her breathing to slow.

'You could nip in and have a look, Jack, make sure she's asleep.'

'I ain't doing that!' Jack looked disgusted. 'There are *rules*, chum. I can't just go around peeking into a lady's bedchamber.'

'Coward.'

When Mum had finally dropped off, Autumn clambered up into the attic, which was cramped and sticky with cobwebs.

'You got a cauldron up there?' Jack called,

hovering by the bottom of the ladder like a security guard.

'Not exactly.' Autumn pushed aside boxes of battered books piled on top of each other. 'Think about it, Jack,' she called down in a stage whisper. 'I have *no idea* about my ghost thing, not really. No idea where it comes from. I've never tried to summon a ghost before. But Mrs Kaur was there when I needed her, you were there when I didn't have any friends . . . do you think it's possible I have some . . . *control* over it? And if I combine it with a magic stone, maybe . . . *a-ha*!' She finally spotted what she was looking for tucked into a corner.

'You know that's your barbecue, right?' Jack peered up with a crinkled forehead.

'It can burn things, can't it?' Autumn said defensively.

They'd had a million summer trips to the local park with the portable barbecue, armed with full shopping bags, a picnic hamper and boules. Dad had insisted on grilling a cabbage whole. There was something appropriate about that barbecue being the thing that brought him back. If it worked.

She scooped up the barbecue, grabbed a bag of

charcoal with her spare hand and carried them both downstairs – making sure to miss the creaky step – and out on to the cliff. There was a good spot at the top of the beach – far enough away so she wouldn't set fire to the house, but close enough that she could go running back inside if she needed to.

'Autumn, listen . . .' Jack halted by the door, taking his cap from his head solemnly. 'I think it's only proper that I leave you and your da alone. Give you a bit of time.'

Autumn looked at him quizzically. 'You sure it's not because you're frightened?'

He coughed gruffly. 'Well . . .'

'Jack, you are *literally* a ghost.'

'But it's not just that. It's a special thing, to love someone like you love your da. I wish I remembered mine. And you deserve your reunion, just you, so leave me here and I'll wait in the chimney till you call.'

She tried to answer but couldn't, so she just nodded and dropped his card on the doormat.

No time to lose, Autumn. Now or never.

39

There was a loud bark from Watchman's Cottage. Bracken's nose was pressed up against the kitchen window, floppy ears pricked.

'*Sssh*, Bracken!' Autumn whispered, doing the best *get out of here* head jerk that she could muster. 'You'll wake The Dog!'

The beagle sniffed and stayed put.

Autumn flew down the cliff steps, the adrenalin that coursed through her veins keeping her warm against the night's chill. She set a torch on the sand and scattered the charcoal inside the barbecue. With a ceremonial breath – she thought that was important, given the significance of the event – she placed Dad's stone in the centre of it.

The matches had been tucked safely inside her

pocket and she reached for them now, pushing down the thought that refused to die. *What if this doesn't work?*

Her hands wobbled as she tried to light the fire, but the match barely sparked before dying again. The second was extinguished by a gust of wind. She covered the third with her palm and it burst into flame, so she placed it into the charcoals and watched with relief as a gentle orange glow lit up the darkness. Bending into the warmth, she blew the embers so that the coals smouldered and shone.

It was time. Mum's curtains were still closed; no light was switched on. She was safe for now.

With clumsy hands, Autumn produced the crushed sea holly from her pocket, trying hard not to shiver.

The herb hissed as it hit the coals and a flurry of smoke blustered into the air. It smelt rich and earthy.

'Now, Autumn,' she muttered to herself. 'Remember who you are.'

She sat on her haunches and pictured all the thousands of ghosts that had ever visited. From Jack, to Christian, to Mrs Kaur and Weltingham and every nameless ghoul that had begged for help. *Wherever my gift comes from,* she thought, eyes tightly shut, *let it call out to him now. Dad. Dad. Dad.*

With a fluttering heart, she sank to the grass and watched the smoke dance in the air and waited for something to happen. For another call of *'find me'*. For Dad to emerge.

She sat there for half an hour before the rain came.

40

The charcoals fizzled and died and the last of the smoke wafted away, taking Autumn's hope with it. She stayed for a few moments longer just in case Dad materialized in the dying embers, but the rain fell in sheets and pummelled the coals to ash, leaving the stone perfect and uncharred and useless. She was alone.

It's OK. Her thoughts were forced as she stashed the barbecue round the side of the house. *It was never going to work. You knew he was gone, really.* She rubbed her eyes with the back of her hand, refusing to let tears fall despite them pressing up against her eyelids with increasing weight.

Bracken yelped through next door's window. 'Didn't work, girl,' Autumn answered. 'Nothing to get excited about.'

She crept to the front door and pushed it open gently so as not to wake Mum. The temperature had dropped so she grabbed the blanket from the sofa, slipped off her wellies and tiptoed towards the stairs, desperate to fall into a dreamless sleep where nothing mattered and nothing hurt.

Goosebumps sprang from her skin.

There was a girl sitting on the bottom step.

'Hallo, miss.'

Autumn stuffed a fist in her mouth to stop herself from crying out.

The girl was young, and wearing a blue, short-sleeved dress with embroidered flowers. She jumped lightly off the step, her chestnut plaits swinging. 'Are you poorly?' The movement wafted a scent of sand and seawater.

'No.' Autumn shoved her hands over her ears and ran up the stairs. 'No, no, no, no, no.' She flung herself on her bed and buried her face in the pillow. It was a ghost. An actual human ghost for the first time on land.

And it wasn't Dad. He was never coming back.

'You sure you're not unwell? Only you look

peaky to me.'

Autumn's body had turned to lead, and it took a monumental effort to roll over and face the worried-looking girl by the door. She was so tired. She didn't have any energy left. 'I'm fine, thank you,' she managed. 'But if you don't mind, I'd like to get some sleep.'

'Course.' The girl broke into a smile. 'I'm not stupid; I'll leave you be.'

Autumn hauled the covers over her head and hid in the darkness.

'But can you help me first?' The voice was closer. The girl was standing right over her.

Of course.

Maybe the spell had worked after all. Right spell, wrong ghost.

'Was it you?' Autumn's voice was close to breaking as realization washed over her like the tide. The seawater smell of the girl. The shadow. The voice from Brae's Rock. 'Did you call "find me"?'

The ghost nibbled the end of her plaits. 'Um, yes?' she said doubtfully. 'I don't know. Maybe? Honest, I don't even know where I've been. Everything's all blurry and forgottening.'

The girl sat next to Autumn on the bed. The unwelcome, familiar presence of a ghost seeking help made Autumn's stomach churn. For the old times, for London, for Dad; Dad, now so far out of reach he might as well have died all over again.

'What is it you want?' Autumn said dully, thinking only of sinking into her pillow and oblivion.

'I need to find my brother. He said he'd find me, only he hasn't and I don't know where to look.'

Find me. Well, that made sense. Her gut clenched.

'What's his name?'

The girl opened her mouth to answer and then shut it again, panic flitting across her face. 'I can't remember. Why can't I remember?' She scrunched her plaits in her fists, then snapped her fingers and let out a whoop. 'Course I remember – what a dullard! He's Will!' She leapt off the bed and pranced round the room. 'And he likes flowers and painting and doing music with me and sea-swimming. We've got a game where I hide things and he always looks, even when he's tired. He's such a good brother, miss, and he was going to find me, but I don't think he knows where to look.'

Autumn's head was pounding. At this point she'd

say anything to get some sleep. 'If I try to help tomorrow, will you leave me alone for now?'

The girl jumped off the bed and saluted. 'You have my word.'

Autumn threw herself back on to the mattress and blocked out the world with her pillow. The girl's voice sounded close to her ear, muffled, but unmistakeably there.

'I'll go and wait downstairs for you. Let you get some rest; happen you'll need your strength to seek out Will. Oh, and afore I forget this too, my name's Lily. Pleasure to make your acquaintance.'

Squeezing her eyes shut, Autumn waited for the scent of seawater to fade. A soft gust of air ruffled her hair and The Dog started barking from the kitchen.

She fell asleep with the pillow over her head, the tears finally sliding down her face.

41

'**M**orning sleepyhead!'

Autumn strained her eyes open to see Lily sitting on her mattress smiling at her. Chestnut plaits and bright blue cloth wobbled around the edges of her vision.

'Sleep well?'

It took a moment for the boulder in her head to move, but slowly the world came into focus and her memory reformed.

Dad's not here. We don't live in London any more. There's a dead girl in my room. Dad's not here. There's no hope left.

She sat up, glimpsing herself in the bedroom mirror with a shudder; her dark curls were lank, her skin pasty and blotchy, and indigo eye bags were the only colour in her face. She looked half-dead.

'You found Will yet?'

'No, Lily. I've been asleep.'

'Course, course.' Lily raised her finger to her lips. 'You eat your breakfast and I'll keep myself busy.'

Autumn's tread down the stairs was heavy and sad, and she forgot to jump over the bottom step. The resounding *creak* seemed crueller than usual. Malicious.

At breakfast, she nibbled a corner of dry toast and wrote a message in her notebook with large, hard letters. Mum was annoyingly energetic, chattering over her blackberry salad about Fred and synapses sparking in the brain, so when her back was finally turned Autumn grabbed the opportunity and whispered to the playing card.

Crack. Jack appeared before she'd even finished his name. 'Love a duck, you know how to keep a lad waiting. Where is he?'

His exuberance hurt. Keeping one eye on Mum and her blackberries, Autumn tapped the corner of the notebook.

IT DIDN'T WORK. DAD DIDN'T COME.
WE'VE GOT ANOTHER GHOST INSTEAD.

'Oh. Oh, chum.'

She ripped the page out. She didn't want his pity. Pity didn't help anyone. The only thing to do was shake her head flatly and point upwards.

'You mean, it's up there now?' Jack pulled the knife from his belt, slicing through the air. Autumn shrugged and forced down her toast. It stuck in her throat and tasted like dirt.

'Are you all right, honey?' Mum blew the steam off her coffee and frowned so hard the glasses slipped down her nose. 'You seem kind of morose today; are you OK?'

Autumn was sick of it. She was sick of trying to go with the flow and drink in the magic. What was the point of any of it?

With a gust of sea-scented air, Lily appeared in the kitchen and Jack yowled like a frightened cat. 'Argh, Autumn, she's looking at me. She's *looking* at me!'

Lily grinned widely, looking like she'd won the lottery. 'Ooh, miss, there's another one like me! A grubby one!' She gave Jack a clear, direct stare. 'Were you down the mines at Redruth?'

'Was I 'eck.' Jack's eyes were squeezed shut in terror.

The Dog had never looked happier; he galloped jubilantly between his two dead friends with his tongue hanging out of his mouth, slamming into furniture and slipping on the tiles. The manic barks of Bracken sounded from next door.

'What's got into him? He's possessed this morning.' Mum sidled closer and Autumn knew she was in for the inevitable arm squeeze and the cocked, concerned head, so she edged out of reach and headed for the door.

'Yeah. Well, I've got to head off. I'm going to see Lamorna.'

Lily and Jack both squeaked, barring the door. 'You can't leave now, miss! What about Will?'

'You ain't got the card, Autumn. Don't leave me here with her!'

'Honey, are you sure you're OK?'

Any minute now, she'd explode. She was sure of it.

'Don't worry, *Mum*,' she said, her eyes shooting fireballs at the two ghosts blocking her way. 'I'll talk to you this evening, all right?'

Lily and Jack nodded in unison, and Mum went back to her fruit. 'Aw, sweetheart,' she muttered sadly. 'We were getting on so well.'

'Bye, miss! I'll be waiting!'

'If she comes near the chimney, there'll be *hell* to pay, chum, *hell* to pay!'

42

Outside, the morning mocked Autumn with its warmth. Endless days of wind and greyness and *now* the sun shone.

She glanced back at the house. Lily and Jack stood by the window, waving their arms joyfully. Pulling her back into a world she'd thought she'd managed to leave.

'Morning!'

Fred was standing outside his front door, cradling a mug of something hot. Autumn waved half-heartedly. 'Morning, Mr Emlyn.'

'Little one, don't be heading out,' he called. 'Stay in. The storm mist. I won't be long at the mainland. Just to the shop and then we'll hole up inside.'

Not sure how to respond, and full to the brim

with *everything*, she waved back. 'There's no storm today, Mr Emlyn. I'll be back soon, I promise.'

He remained rigid. 'Tell Iz you'll be back home afore dark. The flood's a-coming.'

Pushing all her guilt down into the pit of her stomach, she turned her back on him and marched down and round the coiled track, fuelled by anger and injustice and all the things she'd tried not to feel since Dad had gone. She stomped across the harbour in tattered wellies and found Lamorna sitting on the jetty, legs dangling in the ocean.

'Autumn! What a beautiful morning, don't you think? The sea is a millpond today.'

The sight of her real live, breathing friend calmed her slightly. She made a noise that sounded like *humpf* and sat down beside Lamorna.

Neither of them said anything. Apart from the shriek of gulls and the gentle lap of the surf, the two girls sat in silence, Autumn's dark curls next to Lamorna's white-blonde tresses.

'Before I forget . . .' Autumn reached into her bag and pulled out *Spells of the Sea*. 'You can have this one back. I'm done with it.'

Lamorna took it, looking taken aback. 'Oh! This

is the book you chose?'

Autumn nodded, her mouth scrunched into a painful ball.

'My mother adored this book.' Lamorna was quiet. 'She adored the idea of magic, and our myths, too. She was a Mainlander too – although her mainland was much further away. Perhaps magic is more tempting for those who don't grow up on Imber.'

Autumn gave her a sidelong glance. Lamorna seemed even sadder than she did today.

'Anyway. Tush. I hope you enjoyed the book as much as she once did.'

'Mmm.' The idea that she'd even hoped for magic now seemed totally stupid. Of course it hadn't worked.

Lamorna drew patterns in the water with her toe. 'You know, Mother actually tried casting some of those spells. She always claimed that magic never gives you what you want. It gives you what you need. So, for example, if a spell is cast for freedom, or happiness . . .' Her eyes darkened and she turned her head back to the ocean. 'Well, let's just say things come in a way we do not expect.'

They were quiet again. Autumn watched the

fishing boats bob in the water. Blue and white and red. She was sure there used to be more boats moored there. The only ones left were battered and old: *The Cornish Pisky. Älskling. The Dozmary.* That one looked particularly exposed and weather-beaten. Like her.

'I can tell something's worrying you, Autumn,' Lamorna said gently. 'May I make a suggestion?'

'Absotootly.'

'Have you tried music?' Lamorna asked. 'It can calm a troubled soul like nothing else.'

'My dad used to play the banjo when he was stressed.' Just the mention of him made her eyes burn. *Don't cry. Not now.* She tried to focus on a small shoal of fish darting round her toes.

'A number of us come together on occasion to sing shanties by the seafront,' Lamorna continued. 'It's a tradition brought over from the Cornish settlers. Perhaps you'd like to join us?'

Ordinarily, the idea of singing in front of people would have made Autumn's insides shrivel with embarrassment. But she could feel the storm twisting and writhing in her belly, and she suspected she'd need a distraction before she burst.

And Lamorna wanted her there.

'I'd like that,' she said gratefully. 'I've heard some sea-singing already. It's beautiful.'

'Oh, have you?' Lamorna looked at her askance. 'That's interesting.'

'And I promise not to throw tomatoes at anyone.'

Lamorna chuckled, and the storm in Autumn's stomach calmed a bit. 'I am so glad to hear that. I will send the word round and collect you in due course.' With that she stood, brushing pebbles off her skirt. 'You've enlivened my spirits today, Autumn. I'm glad to know you.'

'I'm glad to know you too, Lamorna.'

Autumn hugged her knees to her chest, staying on the jetty long after Lamorna had left – long enough to watch the sun reach the middle of the sky and slide towards afternoon.

She couldn't stop thinking about what Lamorna had said. *Magic never gives you what you want. It gives you what you need.*

It was useless pretending a ghost girl wasn't in her house. Maybe she *was* there for a reason. Annoying as it was, she had to give Lily another chance.

43

'Right, little chum,' said Jack. 'Strangest thing about being dead. Go.'

'Ooh . . .' Lily scrunched up her mouth. 'Not being hungry. I loved a good egg, I did. And jam. And dripping. But now my tum's full all the time, like I've eaten a rock.'

'See, I never ate much anyways,' said Jack. 'It's why I'm such a pipsqueak. Give me a lemon sherbet though and I'm yours for life. Or death.'

At this, they both threw their heads back in laughter. Autumn cleared her throat, feeling suddenly very bulky and full of bones. The last thing she'd expected was for these two to be curled up on the sofa together, chattering like old women at bingo.

And they were making the house colder than the Arctic.

Jack and Lily leapt to their feet with a chorus of *''Ere, you're back! We didn't half miss you!'* and The Dog licked Autumn's shin. They all looked spectacularly pleased to see her. She wished it didn't feel so wrong.

'So, you guys are friends now?'

'You bet your bloomers. Who could be scared of this little one?' Jack grinned, casting a protective eye over Lily. 'We've even got a name for the three of us. The Ghost Gang. What do you think?'

'Um . . . sure. Hey, is Mum out? I thought now might be a good time to chat, Lily. See what you remember.'

Lily shivered with excitement. 'Ooh, really?! Your ma went out just after you did. She was wearing a tunic and carrying a case.'

'Good. Hopefully we've got a bit of time.'

The three of them bundled up the stairs. Lily skipped up two at a time, making happy noises as she landed silently on the wooden steps, and Jack stuck close to Autumn, wearing a new expression. It looked like respect.

'Proud of you, chum,' he whispered. 'You're doing a good thing.'

She swallowed. It felt more like going against everything she'd taught herself. But she'd cast a spell to call Dad. And Lily had appeared. She had to see if it meant something.

Autumn led them into her room, leaving The Dog whining on the landing rug. Lily peered through the gap at the bottom of the door.

'Will he be all right out there? I think he gets frighted on his own.'

'He's fine.' Autumn chose a new notebook from the Christmas present stack on her bookshelf – this one had a picture of a cat dressed like David Bowie on the front – opened the first page with a sigh, and wrote:

FINDING WILL

She settled on the bed, legs crossed underneath her. Jack sat up on the wardrobe, helpfully absconding himself unless called upon, and the fork-and-spoon windchimes tinkled as Lily brushed past them. She bounced on to the mattress into a kneel, displaying grazed, freckled knees that skimmed the hem of her blue dress.

'Who's this then?' she demanded, pointing at John Lennon's face on Autumn's duvet cover.

'That's a band. Musicians called The Beatles, from a long time ago. They were awesome.'

'I like music too,' Lily grinned. ''Specially when they sing songs at the beach.'

Autumn took a thorny breath that scratched her chest.

Let's just say things come to us in ways we do not expect.

'You ready to start?'

44

Lily nodded eagerly and lay on her front, legs bent up in the air behind her and plaits in mouth. Her open face made Autumn feel like a fraud.

'Lily, I haven't really done this before, and I don't really know what to do. I'm sorry if I get it wrong.'

'You're doing grand, chum.' Jack's voice sounded firmly from the top of the wardrobe.

'Why don't we just have a nice talk?' Lily leant forward, her blue eyes earnest. 'That's all it is. Just a chat. Like we're friends. Which we are, aren't we? All of us. The Ghost Gang.'

Autumn tucked a stray curl behind her ear, annoyed by the warm glow in her stomach. It was hard to feel too miserable in Lily's presence; she was a bundle of colour and air that swept through the house like a hurricane. She'd won Jack over, that was for certain. He was chuckling at her like a proud older brother. But Autumn had a *real* friend now. She couldn't get pulled back in.

'OK then. What's your full name?'

'Lily.'

Autumn paused mid-scrawl and looked up. 'You don't have a second name?'

Lily thought for a moment, scrunching up the hem of her skirt until her knuckles turned white. When she released them, she looked crestfallen.

'I'm not sure. Can't remember it if so.' She tugged at one of her plaits fiercely. 'Why can't I remember? What's wrong with me?'

'Honestly, don't worry. Sometimes ghosts don't remember much at all.' Autumn glanced imploringly at Jack.

'S'true,' he obliged, kicking his heel against the wardrobe. 'Once upon a time I couldn't tell you a thing. Nothing that mattered; just flashes. But most popped back. Dunno my name – Autumn gave me this one cos of my card.'

'Oh, cripes, that's true.' She'd forgotten that. 'You see, Lily? It's normal and it may come. Just be gentle with yourself. Take it slow.' Autumn surprised herself with the words that poured from her mouth. She sounded like she knew what she was doing. She sounded like Mum. 'What *do* you remember?'

Lily hopped on to the patchwork rug and flitted to the window, turning her face to the sky. 'I remember planes flying over. I'd never seen planes afore, and there were a ton of 'em swooping through the sky like blackbirds.'

'Go on.'

'I remember flags. I remember shouting and clapping.'

'Good, that's really good, Lily. All this is super helpful.'

Lily was getting into it now. She strode around the room, climbing over the furniture with a far-off gaze. Autumn scribbled and forced herself not to think about Lamorna, and the swimming, and the belonging.

'Will got me a new dress.' Lily looked down at her outfit as if seeing it at last. 'This one, it was! And there was a lot of rain.' She breathed on to the window. No steam appeared on the glass. 'Then it was a bad day. I was scared. Will was near . . . he was calling . . . there was a bell.' She shook her head. 'I just remember all the rain. The water. And then I couldn't see Will any more.'

45

L ily flopped down on the floor and puffed.
'I . . .' She shook her head. 'I'm sorry, miss, I
can't do any more. All this remembering is hard.'

Sensing she'd tired her out, Autumn raised a
loaded eyebrow at Jack who winked in understanding. He leapt off the wardrobe and tapped Lily
underneath the chin.

'Come on, little chum. Let's give the mutt the
runaround, shall we?'

Lily smiled shakily and the two ghosts *swooshed*
through the door, the sound of cheerful barking
accompanying them down the stairs.

Grasping the moment of peace, Autumn fell back
on to her pillow and let the golden beam of sunlight
from the window warm her face. The break of the

waves on the shore was as familiar to her now as the rumble of the tube had been in London, the briny smell of the sea better than the coffee brewing in the greasy spoon beneath their flat.

She belonged here.

'CHUM, YOU COMING?'

She grimaced. Jack's screech pulled her old world back into the new.

She trudged downstairs to see Lily and The Dog playing hide and seek. Jack leant against the stove.

'I'll keep her pecker up, don't worry. Wherever she's been, it ain't been good for her.' He beamed at Autumn. 'You're a natural at coaxing her, chum. It's been your gift this whole time, I reckon.'

'It's just this once.'

'What are you thinking?'

'I don't know.' Autumn sighed. 'I really don't know. My brain is full.' Her shoulders sagged and she leant back against the stove. It was still a bit warm from breakfast.

A chiming from the kitchen clock made her jump in alarm. *Fiddlesticks.* Three o'clock. It wouldn't be long until Mum came home.

'Autumn.' Jack's warning stopped her in her

tracks. 'Don't look at me. Don't talk to me. Hark out there.'

Autumn followed his frightened glare.

Lamorna Hawthorn was outside, staring through their window.

46

'Lamorna!' she called brightly as she hurried outside, Jack hot on her heels. Her throat was tight with panic. 'What are you doing here?'

Lamorna stepped elegantly off the sandbag she was standing on. She blocked out the sun, and the pink glow made her look like an angel.

Autumn glanced at the kitchen window to see Lily gawping out, her mouth in a round 'oh'. By her own side, Jack's whole body was clenched, primed for a confrontation he couldn't make. Lamorna couldn't have come at a worse time.

'Er, so . . .' Autumn tried to keep the fear from bursting out of her, but her hands were trembling uncontrollably. She hid them in her jumper. 'Is everything OK?'

Did she see me talking to myself? Please don't let her have seen me talking to myself.

Before she'd been old enough to hide it, they'd caught her talking to herself. Well, to the plague victim who haunted the Year 2 classroom. The laughs and the pointing, the wide berths and the whispers of *weirdo* followed her through that school and the next and built a wall inside her, brick by brick.

Here was her only living friend in the world, and she might be about to turn on her too. Autumn didn't think she had the strength to lift any more bricks.

Lamorna smiled. 'I'm dreadfully sorry, Autumn. I was simply coming to call for you.'

'Bunkum,' sneered Jack, fists balled. Autumn had never seen him look so cross. 'She was snooping.'

'Call for me?' Autumn ignored him and tried to focus. Her mind was a whirlpool of voices.

'Indeed.' Lamorna offered her wide, sparkling grin. 'For the singing? I've brought Zennor. I thought we might ride down to the sea. We'll be like aristocrats on a promenade.'

Her face was hopeful. Warm. Autumn unclenched

her jaw. *Is it possible?*

Lamorna was still talking to her. Lamorna hadn't spotted anything weird. Lamorna still wanted to hang out with her. She could've cried with relief. 'Oh, yes!' she cried. 'Yes, please. I want to come.'

Jack snorted incredulously. 'Wait, you're going to let her get away with spying on you? Autumn, this ain't right! And you were in the middle of gabbering to me!'

Autumn rubbed her temples and longed for him to read her mind.

I'll be back, I promise. I just need a minute.

Far beneath them, the sea had grown stronger and was crashing into the rocks. It sounded like the voice in her head. Inside the house, The Dog woofed and growled, making crashing noises as he banged excitedly into the furniture. Lily's giggles harmonized with the patter of her footsteps.

'Is everything quite all right in there?' Lamorna peered at the window again, concerned. 'Do we need to check on your dog?'

'No, no. Mum will be home soon. Let's go.' Autumn widened her eyes at Jack and tried to communicate with magical brain waves. *Why don't*

196

you come? Then you'll see it's OK.

If Jack did read her mind, he didn't show it. Instead, he clicked his tongue and kicked the ground with a scuffed boot. 'Lor', I wish I understood you. What was all that about, "just this once"? One minute you're all ready to help Lil, and now you're turning your back on her? I know you ain't never been keen on us lot but that's just cruel, that is.'

That's not what I'm doing! Again, Jack didn't respond, despite her thoughts roaring louder than thunder. He stormed alongside her, matching her pace on the path.

'Chum, I understand you wanting to be normal, course I do, nobody's had it stranger than you. But it don't mean you have to follow this . . .' – he swept his eyes over Lamorna and frowned – 'hornswoggler, just cos her heart beats.'

That did it.

'Lamorna, give me a second.' Her head rapidly filling up with steam, Autumn spun on her heels and marched back to the front door. Jack ran to catch up.

'We'll talk when I'm back.' Autumn spoke

through clenched teeth, annoyed at the fire smell and Jack's hot, angry presence. 'I just need some time.' Ignoring his protests, she took a deep breath and posted the playing card through the letterbox, watching it float like a feather on to the mat below.

'But ...'

Like the *ping* of an elastic band, Jack was pulled sharply back into the house, landing next to Lily who clapped gleefully at his trick.

'Autumn, this ain't right!' Jack shouted through the glass, and icicles sprang from the windowpane. 'You've hitched your horse to the wrong flaming wagon!'

She pretended she couldn't hear him, and instead jogged to the real horse waiting a little way up. Zennor was snow-white and magnificent. Autumn couldn't believe that she was allowed to be near him, let alone ride him, but Lamorna helped her climb up and settle astride Zennor and suddenly she felt taller than the Big House itself. Lamorna sat behind her, slid her arms through Autumn's and took hold of the reins. The warmth of her real-life friend spread into her bones and filled her up.

I belong here.

Lamorna giggled as Zennor's saddle bobbed Autumn up and down – and the two ghosts were left alone, watching them go.

47

A few islanders were gathered in a circle at the seashore, wearing overalls and wellies. Autumn recognized some of them from the pub and they called out as Zennor came to a stop on the sand.

Lamorna helped Autumn dismount. The pink glow of the sunset and the smell of fish made her feel sick. Come to think of it, maybe this hadn't been the *best* decision she'd ever made.

Would they actually expect her to sing? The only time she'd gone on stage was to read a poem written by the ghost of a writer and she'd been disqualified for cheating. *Seven-year-olds don't write rhyming couplets, Miss Albert.*

'Friends!' Lamorna cried. 'I've brought a willing sacrifice!'

The islanders laughed and beckoned the two girls to the water's edge. Fog had settled over the ocean and covered their feet and legs. It was like she was paddling in a sea of mist. Autumn felt Lamorna budge in beside her and she craned to whisper in her ear.

'What happens now?'

'Each takes a turn. Sometimes we sing as a group.' Autumn wondered why Lamorna was trembling. Excitement, probably. It wasn't cold. 'If you wish to join with your own song, you're most welcome and shall not be judged. You're one of us now.'

Autumn gulped and said nothing.

The first islander closed his eyes and launched into a tragic song about a boy from the forge dying in lightning fire. His voice was deep and rich, and sounded as solid as Imber rock.

'"The Ballad of the Blacksmith's Boy",' Lamorna whispered.

The next chose 'Buoyed with Ale and Mirth', a tale of the first Cornish settlers on Imber. She could twist and bend with her voice, so it went high and low, and quiet and loud.

Then it was silent, and they were all looking at her.

'The floor is yours if you wish, Autumn.' Lamorna nudged her shoulder gently. 'Take your time.'

She stood rooted to the spot. The sun was near to setting. Perhaps she could wait until it got dark and then hide in a cave.

'Scared of this too, are we, little maid?' A velvet voice made her jump. Morvoren poked her head out from behind another islander, scarlet shawl crossed over her chest. 'I deigned to join the rabble today . . . when I heard *you* were in attendance.' Her tone was light, but she looked exhausted.

'I'm not scared,' mumbled Autumn.

'Wonderful!' said Lamorna.

The sun finally sank beneath the horizon, sending pink and yellow rays across the water. The islanders became silhouettes. Autumn's breath shot out in steam.

'Come, little maid.' The shape of Morvoren leant towards her and Autumn's nostrils burnt with fire and ocean. 'We all have our own song. Dig deep, and I'll help you find it.'

48

O ne of the islanders held a lamp aloft. Lamorna's face was illuminated.

'What song can you hear with a quiet spirit, Autumn?' she asked.

I've got two noisy ones at home, Autumn thought, her throat desert-dry. *When have I ever had a quiet spirit?*

The ocean. When she'd swum. The silence of the sea muting her noisy thoughts.

'Open your chest, little maid.' Morvoren held her arms out. 'Palms to the sky. Sing to the sea.'

Autumn stretched her arms as wide as Morvoren had and from the alcoves of her soul an old song of Dad's bubbled, one she hadn't heard for years and years because he'd cried after he sang it. She wasn't sure if she still remembered the words.

Just Dad stuff, Autumn, he'd said, trying to laugh it off. *Sometimes Dads cry too.*

All of her grief, her anxiety, the frustration at the chattering ghosts in her house – all of it poured out.

As if wings of a swift were broken
Or petals from a cornflower torn
I am but a ghost of a person
Spread thin from the day I was born

As she sang, Morvoren joined with her in a different note, swimming beneath the melody and flying above it until their two voices became one.

How do I live with the endless noise?
How do I think, or sleep, or be?
Let me dive in the calling ocean
Let me sleep in the warmth of the sea

Her song ended, half-whispered into the fog. When she opened her eyes, the singers had encircled her. They were staring.

'Told you, little maid,' Morvoren said with a

204

smile. 'I'm never wrong.'

'Autumn.' Lamorna was at her side, a gentle hand upon her arm. 'Where did that come from? Have you ever sung before?'

Autumn stood panting for breath, hoping an octopus would appear and pull her into the ocean with its tentacles. 'Er . . .' Where *had* it come from? All the things she'd been hiding – dumped and piled and locked away – had flowed out of her in front of *actual people*.

'No.' She backed further up the shore, her boots vanishing into the mist. 'That was the first time. And the last. Load of old nonsense really.'

The singers burst into excited chatter.

'Wherever it came from,' Lamorna said softly, 'we're honoured to hear it. Music tells a story, Autumn. You have the true soul of Imber.'

Just like Dad.

And for a moment, surrounded by song and friends, it was like he hadn't gone at all.

49

Lily was trying really hard to make everything OK, Autumn could tell. She was pottering round the house with The Dog, pointing out stuff.

'And this is the wireless . . .' (it was the radio). 'Only the Big House was allowed one of them. Then they told us all the news. This is the safe . . .' (it was the fridge), 'and this is where you keep your 'spensive things, like mushrooms.'

Nobody answered. Autumn and Jack stared at each other from opposite sides of the kitchen, daring one another to speak first. He was hurt, Autumn knew that. But she was allowed other friends. He didn't have to get so grumpy about it.

In the end, it was Jack who broke the silence. He held his cap in coal-streaked hands, and Autumn's skin turned icy cold. 'Have a spiffing time with Lamorna?' His voice didn't sound like his.

'Yes, thank you.' Autumn gripped the edge of the sofa with white fingernails. It felt so wrong, talking to him like this and having him shoot bile back at her. He was supposed to be her safe place.

'I thought you was going to help Lily?'

Lily made a nervous squeaking noise and joined The Dog in the doorway. Autumn rolled her eyes in frustration and threw her hands up in the air.

'I will help Lily. I've said I will help Lily. I *want* to help Lily, of course I do, but blimey, can't you just let me have this one thing?'

Jack flitted to her side earnestly. 'Chum, I ain't stopping you doing nothing.' The smell of chimney ash wasn't as comforting as it usually was. 'I only want you to be happy, that's all I've ever wanted. But Lamorna ain't good, Autumn, she's shifty, I swear it – and I think you're walking into something you shouldn't be.'

'Enough!' Autumn yelled, and Lily put her hands over her ears. 'Jack, don't you get it? This is where I belong. It's where I'm *from*. I'm good at things here. I have friends here, real live breathing friends, and it's like you want me to go back to being lonely old Autumn again, just so you can feel like you're not on your own.'

As soon as the words shot out of her mouth, she wished she could stuff them back in.

The chimney sweep fell into shocked silence, and through the angry throb in her head Autumn saw him as he truly was. A scared twelve-year-old boy, forced to go through life – and death – alone.

'Send me back,' he said quietly.

'What?' It was all going wrong. It wasn't supposed to be like this.

He turned his back on her and his voice was small. 'I want to go home. I want to watch the tellybox at Mr Mazur's. I want to listen to Agnieszka blub about her boyfriends. I want to hear the cars outside and smell the cafe downstairs and feel like *I* belong. Cos chum, I don't here.'

He didn't. Cockney and citified in the smoky rags of Victorian London, now dropped in the middle of the Celtic Sea.

'Fine,' Autumn muttered, ignoring the sick feeling of regret that was pooling in her stomach. Lily threw

208

her arms round him and The Dog whimpered at his feet.

'What about the Ghost Gang?' she heard Lily murmur sadly.

'Sorry, Lil,' came Jack's muffled reply into her neck. 'But you don't need me around, ruining things.'

Autumn took the playing card from the mat, running her thumb over the faded, intricate patterns. It had been her constant since she was five years old. Almost as much *her* talisman as his.

'Are you sure about this?' she asked through clenched teeth. *Because I'm not.*

'Yup.' Jack didn't look at her. He stared at his feet, so all she could see was the top of his dirty blonde hair, stuck up in all directions like a chimney brush. 'I want to go home.'

Trying hard not to let her lip wobble, Autumn lifted the card in the air and placed her fingers at the top of it, gathering the strength to rip it in two.

Jack held up a dirty hand. 'Autumn?'

Phew. The relief rained down on her as a torrent. He wasn't going to leave her after all. He couldn't. She'd say sorry, and they'd be best friends again. 'Yes, Jack?'

'Do what you say,' he said, his voice cracking. 'Help Lily.'

Oh.

With a strength she didn't know she had, Autumn tore the playing card in half. The Jack of Hearts was split in two as though fork lightning had struck him and, with splinters of coal sparkling like black diamonds, Jack began to fade. Autumn could see the sofa through his belly.

'Bye, chum.' With a final *bang* and a puff of smoke, he vanished.

And Autumn's chest felt like a burnt-out fire grate.

50

Jack had been gone for seventeen hours, three minutes and forty-five seconds. His ripped playing card lay useless beside her bed, with The Dog's snout resting on it. As hazy sunshine broke through her window, Autumn longed for the clock to rewind and undo everything.

Before disappearing off next door, Mum had attempted to cheer her up with her dancing. 'Fred's been teaching me. Wanna join in?' She stomped on the rug as if she were crushing grapes, arms sweeping through the air. Autumn knew she should make her happy, knew she should twirl and laugh and reassure her that they were still friends. But she didn't because it was all too much effort.

'Yeah, Mum, great. See you later.'

'Miss . . . ?' Lily followed her sombre trajectory through the kitchen, twiddling her plaits nervously. 'You must miss the sweep something dreadful. But you haven't forgotten about Will, have you? You'll try and find him? I can have a think about what I remember if that's helpful?'

Autumn turned away from Lily's earnest face and opened the door. Her dungarees felt hot and uncomfortable in the moist fog. 'Of course, Lily. I promise.' She tapped her notebook, snug in her dungarees pocket, though she felt as helpful as a chocolate teapot. 'I won't let you down. I'll be back, I promise. I just need some air.'

Her thoughts were an angry enemy as she trudged down the steps to the beach. The thick mist hung over the morning like a wool blanket, but she followed the salty brine smell to the shore.

Somebody was swimming, slicing through the water with confident strokes. It looked like they'd come from the wild half of the island.

Eyes narrowed, Autumn took small steps forwards until seawater reached her ankles. She could just see the swimmer through the fog, passing the pool of water that ran up the beach. Grey hair ducked in and out of the sea.

'Wow, Mr Emlyn!' she shouted in surprise. 'Fred, hey!'

He didn't hear her. His pace picked up, and with a few more easy strokes he followed the island's curve towards the harbour. She couldn't believe how well he could swim. He'd always seemed younger than his years, but his strength was *astonishing*. Before she had a chance to call his name again, he'd disappeared into the mist.

'Autumn, is that you?' A different voice ripped through the fog. Behind her.

'Lamorna?' Autumn shouted back. 'Where are you?'

The tinkling bell laugh. 'Follow the fire! Towards the caves!'

Relieved to be dragged away from her own thoughts, Autumn followed the sea stream's journey to the caves. A pinprick of orange danced ahead and Autumn found her friend sitting on a rock at the cave's mouth, the darkness inside glowing with beams of light. Two circles of wire were clasped in Lamorna's hand, plaited with greenery.

'What a happy coincidence!' Lamorna offered a

radiant grin. 'I was shortly about to call for you.' She held up a plaited circle. 'I've been making these.'

'Blimey, Lamorna,' said Autumn, taking it with careful fingers as if it were made of glass. It was a flower crown – sort of – entwined with deep green seaweed and russet leaves, red berries dotted between. 'They're beautiful. What are they for?'

'Almost beautiful.' Lamorna rose to her feet. 'It needs just one more twist. Would you finish it?'

Autumn wrapped a loose tendril of seaweed round the frame. 'Like that? I don't want to ruin it.'

'Now it's perfect.' Lamorna lifted the crown from Autumn's hands and lowered it on to her curls, then placed the other on her own head. 'Made by both our hands. A part of both of us.'

'What's going on?' Autumn whispered, awed by the weight of it.

With a mysterious ghost of a smile, Lamorna took Autumn's hand in hers and led her over the rocks and into the cave. 'Why, this is all for you.'

51

The cave was smaller than she remembered. Moss-drenched and black, with silhouettes of stalactites hanging from the cave roof like icicles. Orange-flamed torches were wedged between rocks, and they bounced sea-splattered light off the water.

Autumn stood awkwardly at the mouth of the cave. 'What's going on?' She didn't know what to do with her hands.

'A crown of seaweed, for the island and your swim.' Lamorna was by her side, a hint of rosewater. 'Autumn leaves for you. For me, berries of the hawthorn tree. We're friends now. This makes it official.'

'Lamorna . . .' The swelling in her chest made it hard to speak. The only friendship bracelet she'd ever been given was from Mum, which was embarrassing to say the least. In her wildest dreams, she couldn't have expected this. 'I . . .'

The low *tip-tap* of old rain dripped through the cave ceiling.

'Wait a moment – there's more,' Lamorna said, and there was a rustle of activity as she disappeared into the darkness. She returned quickly, clutching something small, hidden by shadow and cloth, and placed her hand in Autumn's. The weight of something unknown landed on her palm.

'In your palm lies a gift of Imber's shores.' Lamorna's voice dropped to a gentle hush. In the firelight she looked as tall as a goddess. 'It symbolizes that you belong to us, and we belong to you. Tied inexorably to one another. One of Imber.'

Autumn kept her eyes locked on Lamorna's. 'One of Imber,' she whispered.

'Are you ready to see your gift, friend?' Lamorna whipped her hand away with a flourish.

Autumn said nothing. The words died on her tongue.

It was a stone with a perfect hole through the centre of it, so precise it could've been drilled. Identical to

Dad's. It shone in her palm, perfect and hers.

It didn't matter if he was never coming back. It didn't matter what his secrets had been. They were connected: by stone, by music, by island.

She squeezed it and felt the warmth of belonging heat her skin. 'Thank you,' she said, although it didn't seem enough. 'Thank you.'

52

'Daughter!' From the fog emerged a familiar face, wiggling with joy. Lord Hawthorn shuffled closer, struggling to keep upright over the wet rock. Old-fashioned binoculars swung round his neck. 'Do I spy the traditional Imber coming-of-age ceremony? Your very first? And without *me*?'

His daughter growled under her breath. 'Go back to looking for puffins, Father.'

Lord Hawthorn, green as samphire in his tweed suit, clapped his hands over his mouth in mock submission. 'Dear me, yes. One mustn't interfere. I presume, Lamorna, my dear, you have shared the tale of the witchstone?'

Witchstone. Autumn looked at it with new eyes. So that was the name of it. It sounded mystical. Important.

Lamorna sat heavily on a flattened ledge. 'You know I did not. I'll wager you've been out there listening for your cue.'

The atmosphere had grown staler. Autumn wondered if she should sneak out and let them get on with it.

'Well, I do relish it so . . .' Lord Hawthorn seemed not to hear the venom in Lamorna's tone. He slid along the rock slightly so he was plunged into the spotlight of a flame. 'All children of Imber receive this gift when they come of age, Miss Albert. It stays with them for the entirety of their natural life.' He paused.

'And then what, sir?' Autumn asked, because she felt like she ought to.

'And upon their death, Imber lore requires their stone to be placed upon the Witchstone Towers.'

Oh. Autumn's thoughts darted like floating dust. The piles of stones weren't fairy stacks at all. They were a shrine to the dead.

She felt the weight of Dad's own stone in her pocket. No wonder he'd kept it so safe all these years. It was always meant to come back home.

Her first thought was to call Jack; to tell him what

it all meant. And then she remembered.

'Did you hear me, Miss Albert?' Lord Hawthorn's voice was sugary-soft. He hopped closer, lowering his bald head so it almost touched hers. The smell of cigar smoke scratched at her nose, and she leant back as far as she could without offending. 'There is one more tradition we keep. A preposterous thing, in truth. But we are fond of it.'

'OK,' said Autumn, wondering what was coming next.

'Once we've been gifted our witchstones,' Lamorna swept in front of her father like a welcome breeze, 'we look through the centre of it. Some islanders swear they see something on the other side.'

Autumn felt her arm gently guided upwards by Lamorna, her hand lifted to her face. The two Hawthorns were staring at her expectantly, eyes twinkling with the same watchful gaze.

Note to self: never tell Lamorna she looks like her father.

Imagining her own dad doing the same thing gave Autumn the push to hold the stone to her eye and peer unblinking through the hole. It framed the cave with light grey.

Lord Hawthorn was so near, it was almost as if he wanted to look through the stone himself. 'Do you see anything, Miss Albert? How do you feel?'

The truth was, she saw the dark hulk of the cave wall. The orange flames. The wibble of the inlet. Just in case, she turned in the direction of the cave's mouth but there was nothing there except impenetrable mist. The more she stared, the less she saw. Had everyone else felt this daft?

'Autumn?' Lamorna's voice was edging on strained. 'Anything?'

She swallowed.

OK, Autumn, you have two options.

Lie. But you suck at lying.

Tell the truth. Brace yourself for the disappointment.

'Um,' she said finally. 'No?'

221

53

In the time it took for a heart to beat, Lord Hawthorn's eyes whipped to Lamorna and back to Autumn again.

'I see.' He grew shinier. Redder. He tugged his beard until it looked like he might rip it off. 'I see.'

Autumn was suddenly ghostly cold.

'Well, time rushes on.' He turned his back on her and gathered the flaming torches in one hand. With a forceful stab, he thrust them all in the water where they were extinguished with a *hiss* and a cloud of acrid smoke. The cave was plunged into black.

'Lamorna?' Her friend had slipped into the shadows, the whites of her eyes wide. Autumn had a feeling she'd done something very wrong. 'Are you OK? You don't look right.'

There was a humourless laugh from the darkness. Lord Hawthorn eclipsed the cave mouth with his silhouette, rigid as a statue. 'Tush. Nothing to concern yourself with, Miss Albert, my dear. I only wish to have the *teensiest* chitter-chatter with my daughter. Lamorna?'

'Of course, Father.' Lamorna's voice was barely there.

'All right,' Autumn said. Panic rose to the back of her throat like a tidal wave. 'Lamorna, I'll wait for you outside, OK?'

'Very well,' came Lamorna's faint reply. Autumn stumbled out as fast as she could without tripping, relieved to breathe lighter air.

As soon as she felt her boots hit sand, she held the stone to her eye again. There was nothing but the cream-thick fog and the blurry shape of Brae's Rock in the distance. She pulled off her seaweed crown sadly and lowered herself on to a rock.

Failure. Loser.

Alarmed by the tears promising to explode, she grabbed her Bowie-cat notebook from her pocket and scribbled everything she'd learnt.

'What are you writing?' Lamorna sounded like

tinkling bells again. She crouched next to Autumn, her pale hair swallowed by the fog. Her nose and eyes looked red and sore.

'Nothing.' Autumn shut her notebook quicky and stuffed it back into her pocket. 'It just . . . helps me organize my thoughts. Are you OK? Did I do something wrong?'

'Autumn, I'm *so* sorry if we worried you,' Lamorna said earnestly, clutching Autumn's hand in hers. 'My father's moods. He ruins everything. Not related to you in the slightest, I promise.' A crease appeared on her forehead. 'I miss . . . I miss my mother more often these days.'

'I'm so sorry, Lamorna. Do you want to talk about it? I mean, that is . . . if you still want to be my friend? Even though I didn't see anything through the stone?'

A flash of something passed across Lamorna's face. Perhaps it was sadness, because she swept Autumn into a bear hug, almost crushing her ribs.

Autumn had never loved being touched for long periods of time. It made her skin hurt. But she didn't mind it now.

'You're a good person.' Lamorna pulled away and

thrust her hands into her coat pockets. 'You belong here. Remember that.'

The relief was staggering. Suddenly Autumn wasn't so cold.

'Thanks, Lamorna. You're a good person too.'

The sad-eyed girl turned her head away and stared at the horizon. 'Nobody's told me that in a long time.'

54

The moon would have been brighter were it not for the endless fog, but Autumn wasn't worried. She'd got the torch, and strong boots. Mum had fallen asleep on the sofa – returning to work had exhausted her and she was usually snoring by nine o'clock – but Autumn kissed her on the forehead and whispered the plan in her ear. She wouldn't hear it, but a part of her should know.

'Mind if I take The Dog?' Autumn poked her head round the bedroom door to see Lily ruffling his fur on the rug. 'Time for his night wee.' She wanted a bit of company, even if it was canine.

Lily chucked herself on to Autumn's bed, one stocking crumpled to her ankle. 'Course, miss. He needs his fresh air, bless him. But you be careful out.

The storm mist is here.'

'At least there's no more rain.'

'Aye, but the storm mist comes before the worst of all.' Lily's eyes glazed over for a moment. 'You need your wits about you when the storm mist comes.'

It's not so bad, Autumn thought as she twisted up and round the island road, her torch leading the way with a golden fuzz. The Dog, however, lifted each paw gingerly as though he were treading on hot coals. Mordros Lane was unnervingly silent. The whitewashed houses were half-hidden by the fog, windows dark. It wasn't that late. Why were there so few lights on? Even The Sea Witch's Rest looked empty.

Climbing down the steps was harder in the misty darkness; she almost lost her footing and eventually just launched herself on to the cliff shelf, landing on her bum with The Dog splayed at her feet.

At least nobody was around to see that.

Even the church bell was quiet. The air was too still.

The sky was navy, and the stone towers glowed like noiseless ghosts. She'd chosen the one nearest to a hawthorn tree. That way, Dad could hear the dawn chorus and birdsong at sunrise. Morning had always found him at an open window, wearing a goofy grin.

Listen to the pigeons, Autumn. They're plotting our demise.

They reached the tower and The Dog readied to cock his leg.

'Not there, mutt,' she said, and he leapt back as if stung by a jellyfish.

She clutched Dad's witchstone in her hand. It felt comfy there. She didn't want to let it go. It was part of him – really the last part she had left apart from the photo – but he deserved the traditional Imber farewell. Wherever his ghost had been, maybe this would help him find his way home.

'So, Dad.' She was glad of the cover of the mist. It hurt to speak. 'This is it, I think. I did try to go with the flow and drink in the magic – enjoy the parts of your soul you left behind – but I wasn't very good at it. I couldn't accept you'd gone. Maybe this is where your breadcrumbs led.' With trembling fingers, she held the stone nearer to the tower. There was a *buzz* of electricity as it grew closer. A zing, like blue lightning, just like she'd felt at Brae's Rock. 'I really hope you'll be happy here, Dad. And I'll come and visit you every day. I love you.'

The Dog howled the same howl he did outside Dad's office. His heartbreak howl. He was like a wolf, crying to the moon.

With the hardest breath she'd ever taken, Autumn forced her eyes shut and placed Dad's stone on the top of the tower, her skin brushing against the stones piled beneath.

And suddenly, she wasn't there any more.

55

Sand crunched beneath her feet, the tang of salt on her tongue. Somehow Autumn was down at the beach, watching two children dressed in old-fashioned swimming costumes play hide and seek in the coves.

'Don't peek, Elowyn!' one child cried, skipping behind the rocks.

Autumn tried to call out but she was voiceless, before suddenly she found herself in a different place altogether.

A shining, unbroken church, with harmonious voices singing and rain hammering the stained-glass windows. Hair was teased into tight buns. A young man sat nervously beside a girl, his bow tie quivering...

'What—'

Once more her voice was swallowed up into the void, and she was in someone's bread-scented kitchen, listening to the kettle whistle on the stove . . .

Then she watched helplessly as families ran from a flood, clambering to the highest ground they could reach as waves licked the cliffs . . .

Then, finally, just as she thought she'd burst open from all the voices in her head, she was back on her own solid ground, curled up on the rocky ledge with The Dog drooling on her face.

What on earth just happened?

Autumn lay unmoving on the ground, compelling her breath to slow. The witchstones towered above her.

The Dog whimpered and Autumn forced herself to her feet. Her head was pounding, swimming with noises and lights that wouldn't settle. Folding her coat over her hand so as not to brush the towers with her skin again, she grabbed Dad's witchstone back and launched herself unsteadily into the mist.

'Lily!' Autumn's whispered scream was hoarse. Her vision was wobbly, and she thought she might throw up. Mum snored gently from downstairs.

'See, miss?' Lily was pale. Worried; pointing out the window with a white finger. 'The storm mist is here. Will always told me to stay inside when the storm mist was here. It's a-coming.'

Autumn pulled her bedroom door ajar, heart thumping. 'Lily, I've got an idea. I've got to ask you something.' Her fork-and-spoon windchimes jangled in the dull wind sneaking through the window gaps. 'Did you have a witchstone too?'

The ghost clutched the skirt of her dress, dark freckles almost floating against her drawn face. It looked like it hurt her, trying to remember. 'Witchstone? Is that . . . *oh*.' Her eyes grew as big as saucers. She leapt on to Ringo Starr and the bed creaked. 'Yes! I had a special stone, miss, what the Big House gave to me, I think. Is that it? Will had one too. Why the asking?'

Autumn paced across her patchwork rug, the fabric wearing thin beneath her boots. 'Because I seem to have this *thing*, I don't know, maybe it's part of my seeing ghosts or something, but I just accidentally touched some of the stones on a tower. And I think . . . when I touch a person's witchstone, I can see their lives. In a flash.'

Lily gaped at her. 'Eh?'

'And it's got me wondering . . . *you're here*. And there are no other ghosts on this island, *none at all*, and maybe that's because putting their stone on the stone towers makes them cross over, like he said in the cave.'

'Who said what?'

'And if you're still here, that must mean that your witchstone isn't on a tower. And if it works like a talisman' – her voice was getting higher with excitement – 'then your stone must be somewhere nearby, because ghosts can't leave their talisman. If we can find it, maybe I can see into *your* life. Maybe I can find Will.'

See, Jack? The warm firefly glow returned to her chest. *I keep my promises.*

56

Autumn barely slept. It didn't help that Lily was making excited little *ooh* noises from the window, but mostly it was because she was holding Dad's witchstone to her skin, willing herself to see something. Anything. But apart from catching the odd strain of *the iron, lads, pull it lads*, Autumn remained very much in her own bed.

Why couldn't she see anything in his witchstone? Had she got the whole thing wrong? If the stone did work like a talisman, shouldn't Dad's ghost be here too?

Her night fears dwindled with the sunrise, in that way her anxiety often did. Maybe the stone's magic only worked for people who'd died on Imber. Maybe Dad's time on the mainland had dulled its power, leaving behind only the smallest echo. That had to be it.

Maybe.

She was trying to eat breakfast when Mum bundled her into a clumsy morning hug. 'Honey, I feel like I haven't seen you in an age. I miss you.' She was bright-eyed and cheerful, smelling of raspberry tea and shampoo. 'Why don't we all hang out today, huh? I'm off on a walk with Fred, then they're both coming over for brunch. Did you know they've never heard of brunch?'

'How is Fred, Mum?' Autumn asked, one eye on Lily dancing with The Dog. 'He seems so healthy. But also, not. Do you know what I mean?'

'Yeah, he's healthy all right. Beth said he's been swimming every day recently. He's as strong as an ox. Physically, he's in the best dang nick I've seen for his age – but that's the cruel trick of it.' Mum pushed her glasses up her nose and slipped on her tunic. 'How scary to know that however fit you are, your brain, your thoughts, your memories – everything that makes you *you* – are being snuffed out like dead matches. He's an extraordinary guy, Fred. I don't think he'll go gently, and that's not necessarily a good thing.'

By the time Mum left for next door, Lily looked ready to explode. 'Is it time, miss? Can we find it now? Can we?'

'We haven't got long. Let me grab my notebook. There might be a clue in what you told me.' Autumn took a hurried glug of juice and rushed upstairs. Truthfully, she was almost as excited as Lily.

She turned her dungarees upside down so that bits fell out of her pocket: an old tissue, some shells she'd collected by the beach, a scrawled note from Mum to remember to buy loo paper, but the notebook wasn't there.

That's weird. When did she last have it? She vaguely remembered scribbling after the ceremony in the cave, and then her memories sank into a black hole. She rummaged around her room and all her usual spots – the box of bits, underneath her pillow, the window seat. But it was nowhere to be seen.

She tried not to panic. It'd turn up when she least expected it.

'Right, change of plan,' she announced as she hurried down the stairs, sounding calmer than she felt. 'Let's try and remember what you said. There were planes, and flags, and clapping. Could it have been the end of the war? Your dress could be from that time . . .'

'Aye!' Lily answered quickly. 'There was a big party. Oh, miss! I'm starting to remember things!'

Autumn grinned at Lily's proud glow. 'Lily, that's amazing! What else do you remember?'

Lily threw herself on the sofa and stuck her tongue through her teeth. 'Just flashes, like the sweep said. Sort of muddy pictures. I remember Will used to sell his paintings on the mainland. A shop in Sennen took 'em, though we never got much for 'em. Right good they were – he painted the sea, and portraits, and all sorts. Oh, and I remember the shanties about mermaids and their lost children, and hiding things in the rock pools, and—'

'Wait, Lily!' A small, insignificant memory burst to life. '*Of course*. You hid things a lot, right?'

'Aye,' Lily nodded. 'It was a game I played with Will. I got so good at it, too. All over the island. There were *so* many things he never found, miss, like the eggcup in the hawthorn, and the paintbrush in the cave.'

A slow smile crept across Autumn's face. Perhaps she and Lily were more alike than she'd thought. 'I've got an idea where to look.'

57

Autumn got a pair of gloves from the cupboard. Just in case.

'So, I hid Jack's playing card behind a brick,' she jabbered as she ran her eye over the stair runner. It was pinned down with rusty nails. 'Nobody thinks of looking in the walls. Dad knew that too.'

Lily and The Dog peeked over the sofa with identical expressions. Eyebrows up, mouths open.

'My special stone is in a wall?' Lily cocked her head in confusion. So did The Dog.

'Not exactly.' Autumn scraped her curls into a messy top knot. 'But I'll bet you had the same sort of idea.'

It took four attempts with the claw edge of a hammer to pull out the first nail. She was horribly aware of the ticking of the clock, of Mum and the Emlyns shortly about to traipse in from the fog for tea and toast. One mighty tug, and the nail came free. Then the same with the others, three on each side. The bottom of the runner came loose, flapping off the step.

Autumn wiped the sheen of sweat from her forehead. 'If this is all for nothing, I'm going to be in *so* much trouble.' She lifted the runner, revealing the step beneath. Despite the dust, the mahogany gleamed brighter than the edges of the staircase.

'I don't understand, miss.' Lily was by her side, peering over her shoulder. The Dog put his snout against her knee.

There was a thin gap between the bottom step and the one above it. Just big enough to hide something small.

'There was a teacher ghost in my old school.' Autumn slipped her hand through the gap and felt around, hoping no spiders were lurking in wait. 'She promised to ignore me if I paid attention in science. So I did. We had this lesson once on Occam's razor.'

'Whose razor?'

Autumn's gloved fingers landed on something

wedged in the corner of the space under the bottom stair. Her sight blurred, and her heart flew into her mouth. 'It's the idea that the right answer is usually pretty simple. Do you remember where you were sitting when you first appeared?'

'Um. The bottom step?' Lily sounded far away.

'The bottom step.' Forcing back the vision that tried to engulf her, Autumn twisted the object between her fingers, coaxing it out gently until it popped through the gap. It fell on to her palm. It was smaller than Dad's. Smaller than hers. Browner, more scratched. A stone with a hole in the middle, as if someone had taken a burning hot poker and stabbed it. 'Next to your talisman.'

'Oh, miss.' Lily's voice was ragged. 'My special stone.' She reached for it hungrily but her pale hand slid through it like water.

Autumn placed it on the arm of the sofa and sank to her knees. 'That's the only step that creaks. It's as if the house was trying to tell us where it was.' It was a strange thing to admit, but she felt a bit proud of herself. She longed for Jack to have seen it too.

Spiffing work, chum. That's what he'd have said.

There came a groan of door hinges, followed by a

flurry of footsteps and voices outside the window.

'Cripes, they're coming!' Autumn lay the runner back in place. No time to attempt a re-nailing. She flailed around for something, anything to make it look less flappy, finally tucking two of Mum's cacti at the back of the step. It'd have to do.

She heard the kitchen door open, and then a stream of cold air burst in.

'Ooh!' said Lily. 'New friends!' The Dog yelped at her excitement and leapt off the floor.

'Lily, I'm so sorry,' Autumn whispered urgently as she heard bustling in the kitchen. 'Can you wait upstairs? He won't settle otherwise. We'll do this later, I promise.'

Lily pulled a face but *swooshed* upwards in a cloud of sea-scented dust, followed swiftly by The Dog. Autumn exhaled in relief.

'Honey?' Mum poked her head into the living room. Her coat was splattered with raindrops. 'I need a quick word with Beth in the kitchen. Fred's going to come and sit in here, OK?'

'OK,' Autumn said, stuffing the gloves up her jumper. 'Awesome.'

Fred didn't look happy as he ducked through the

doorway. His jaw was clenched, and his eyes had the same distant glaze they'd had last time he'd visited. He wriggled uncomfortably as he strode in. It was as if the room made him itchy.

'Want to sit down, Mr Emlyn?' Autumn offered.

Fred flinched. 'I would,' he said quietly, 'it's only that . . .' His words shrivelled into nothingness as he lost them. 'Most kind. Thank you.'

With two giant strides he was across the room, his fleece smattering rainwater on the floor. 'Sorry for the mess,' he grumbled. 'It's pouring—' He stopped mid-sentence and gripped the back of the sofa.

'Mr Emlyn?' Autumn said, alarmed. 'Do you feel all right?' She followed his eyeline to the sofa's arm.

To Lily's witchstone.

58

'Oh . . .' Autumn scrambled for an explanation. 'That's just . . . that's mine. I found it on the beach.'

A pause, and then Fred's tanned face broke into a smile as big as the ocean. 'Found it, my foot!' he boomed. 'You've been gifted your witchstone, haven't you?'

His accent was broader than it usually was. Was he with her, or with someone else? It was so hard to tell. She hesitated, not sure how to answer, but he settled himself down on the sofa and smacked his knees with a large hand.

'It's a special day when you come of age, little one. Come and sit afore the fire and I'll tell you the tale of the Imber witchstones.'

The grate was empty and unlit, but Autumn sat obediently by his feet and joined his world of flames crackling in the hearth; a room cosy with firelight.

Fred turned the stone over and over in his hands, artfully twisting it between his fingers. 'On Imber, we call these a witchstone. They call 'em hag stones on the mainland, or an adder stone. Or a witch stone, two words. This 'ere hole's made by the sea crashing through it.'

'Are they all this size?' Autumn asked, thinking of Brae's Rock.

'Aye, most. Think of the strength it'd take for water to push through that. But you can get bigger ones too. Large as a house. If it's been broke by the tide, it's a witchstone. And it's special.'

'Special how?' The light dimmed through the windows. Rain smacked heavier on the glass.

'People believe a lot of things about these things, little one,' Fred muttered. 'Some reckon you can see magic things through 'em. Some reckons it gives us power over witchcraft or the dead. Like it controls them. And that's wrong. It's not what it's for. Evil people believe evil things.'

Autumn glanced anxiously to the kitchen door, but the murmur of Mum and Beth's conversation was still in full flow.

'What do *you* think it's for, Mr Emlyn?' she whispered. Fred stopped flipping the stone and held it between his thumb and forefinger, staring right through the stone's hole at Autumn so she could see the bright sea-blue of his iris.

'We all get one, us born on Imber. When we're little. It's with us from when we come of age till the moment of our death. We believe our soul is split in twain. Half in here.' He tapped his chest. 'And the other half in there.' He nodded at the stone.

There was a yelp and a loud *crash* from Autumn's bedroom. Fred's head jerked to the ceiling.

'Mr Emlyn!' Autumn said as loud as she dared. 'Tell me, what happens to the stone when we die?'

When Fred looked back at her, his face was as dark as the gathering storm clouds. 'We're told to put 'em on the Witchstone Towers. Then they can cross over. But if you want to keep someone close to you, you keep their stone after they've gone. Then they never leave you.'

Autumn gazed at the stone's hole until her vision

went double. If Lily's witchstone had sat hidden inside the staircase for nearly eighty years, why had she only appeared after Autumn summoned her? Where had she been this whole time?

59

A crack of thunder shook the house, so loud and near that it made Autumn's ears ring. Fred barely moved.

'It's beginning,' he said softly, as lightning blanched the room.

'Mr Emlyn?' Autumn wondered if she should call Mum, but Fred didn't look on edge.

His face was as untroubled as a child's.

'What was I saying?' he muttered, before looking down at the stone in his hand. He stroked it with his thumb. 'Why, this is yours, little one, not mine. What am I doing hogging it?'

'No, Mr Emlyn . . .' Autumn began, but not before he'd put the stone in her palm and folded her fingers over it. The moment her skin touched the surface there was a plume of smoke and she was sitting in her own bedroom, but the walls were different and lighter rain pattered the window.

A small figure leapt down from the bed, chestnut plaits slapping the back of her neck.

Lily.

Autumn tried to call out, but with a painful yank she was pulled back into the present with a view of the ceiling beams. She was splayed out on the floorboards. The stone had rolled under the sofa.

Fred was watching her keenly, wearing a look she couldn't read.

'Brunch time, you two.' Mum appeared through the door with a pale-faced Beth behind her. 'Old man, you've not lived till you've tried my mushrooms on toast.'

Autumn glanced at Fred and could swear she saw an indiscernible nod, so she slipped a glove back on and scooped up the stone. The old man rubbed his face with giant hands and followed Mum into the kitchen. 'I'll be back soon, little one. Tell Iz you'll be back home afore dark. The flood's a-coming.'

*

Mum insisted they both fetch more sandbags for their door, so it was evening before Autumn had a chance to be alone with Lily. She was pleased to get into her warm, comfortable clothes: an old stripy jumper and jeans with seahorses sewn on to the pockets. Dad had bought them from a market in Ely. *Just looks like you*, he'd said.

She switched the main light off and lit her apple and cinnamon candle. Long, looming shadows grew from the flames, and the room filled with the smell of Christmas. It made her feel a bit less terrified.

I wish Jack were here.

'Miss?'

'Yes, Lily?'

'What's going on in that noggin of yours?'

Autumn put a hand to her chest. Her heart felt like it was knocking at her ribcage. 'I think you lived in this house.' She placed the stone on her bed. 'I guess you hid your witchstone in the staircase as part of your game with Will, right? Like the eggcup in the hawthorn tree. And you never got it out again, so it must have been hidden . . .' She let the sentence hang.

'. . . just afore I died.'

'I think so. Sorry, Lily.' Autumn settled on the

bed, trying to block out the roar of the ocean and the distant ringing of the church bell. 'Once I've found out what happened to Will, I'll put your stone on a tower. If it's what you want. My dad's too.'

She rested her head against the pillow and tried to force herself to relax. 'I don't know how long I can go under for. Or how much I'll see. But . . .' She paused, unused to expressing herself. 'But I'm a bit scared, actually. Will you stay with me?'

Lily climbed on to the bed so that her scraped knees were almost touching Autumn's. There was something so familiar about her open expression. 'I'm not going nowhere, miss. We're friends, aren't we? I'm staying right by your side.'

Autumn couldn't answer. She was too near crying for comfort. 'Right then,' she managed. 'Shall we get started? Hope this works, or I'm going to look a right idiot.'

One tree at a time, my love. Never think of the whole forest.

Dad's words echoed painfully as her hands closed round the stone and she was swept into the air with a flash of chestnut light.

60

'Will left a present for you, darling.'

Autumn was as dizzy as if she'd been caught in a tornado. She shook her head and tried to focus, but it was all blurry. Where was she? The room was dark-beamed, grey with rain-light and clouds. Small. Familiar. There was a chest of drawers beside her and she went to lean on it, but her arm went straight through it and she fell to the floor.

She was ephemeral as a ghost. More so. She couldn't even touch the furniture. This thought made her seasick.

'Ma! He didn't!' A small, blurry figure ran towards an older woman. That's when Autumn recognized her own room. It was sparser, with only a compact wooden bed and eiderdown, a sink, the chest of drawers and the same fireplace, decorated with wonky drawings of shells and flowers.

And now her head was swimming back into place she could see that the blurry figure was Lily in a brown, shapeless pinafore, running towards the new dress laid out on the bed: blue, short-sleeved, with embroidered flowers. The dress she would die in.

'He left a note. *Special treat, little one*, he wrote,' said the woman. '*Now you're mixing with them lot at the Big House.* I'd get downstairs if I were you; Isolde's outside, and Will left you stargazy pie.'

'Izzy!' Lily whooped and followed her mother out of the room like an excited puppy. Her loud, cheerful voice flew up the stairs behind her. 'Maybe we'll go rain swimming again! Last time I got to Brae's Rock, can you credit it, Ma?'

Lily was so . . . *bright*. That was the only word Autumn could think to describe her. The life burst out of her like sunshine.

Thunder growled and the windows flew open with a *crash*, letting in a torrent of rain. The world swirled like oil on water and before Autumn could get her thoughts straight, she was lifted high into the air and swept into another room.

Their kitchen. Only the stove was new, the furniture was different and dappled moonlight glittered through a latticed window. It looked like hours had passed.

Lily was in her new dress, lying on her front with her knees kicked up in the air. She tinkled on her penny whistle, a pretty melody that leapt about like the shanties. Another girl, about the same age, was sat primly next to her, hands in her lap. Her clothes were neat. Crystal clean. Next to her, Lily looked like a chaotic scramble. Autumn grinned.

'What about now, Lil?' The neat girl's voice was clipped. Refined. 'Is your mother here now?'

Lily flipped over on to her back and stuck her legs in the air, kicking like she was riding a bicycle. Her plaits were splayed behind her. '*No*, Izzy. I told you.' She droned colourlessly, like she was bored of talking about it. 'She's upstairs. She doesn't come down when others are here in case I talk to her. She says not to tell anyone I see her cos her stone should be on the tower, but you don't count, do you, Iz?'

What?

If Autumn had been in the real world, her legs would have given way.

Was Lily's mum a ghost?

Had Lily been like her?

61

Before Autumn could grasp the thoughts that flew untethered, the air twisted and spun again, and a scene was formed from smoke. The cave from the ceremony with Lamorna, but this time there was a younger, excitable Lily wearing a too-large seaweed crown and proudly holding her new witchstone between her fingers. Isolde was there too, smaller, and hiding behind a tall man with Lord Hawthorn's twinkly grey eyes.

'My dear, you have been clasped to the island's bosom,' he announced in a stately manner. Somebody snorted.

'Bosom,' Lily said, her eyes laughing.

'We ask you to look through the centre of the stone and tell us what is revealed.'

With her tongue stuck between her lips, Lily nodded and placed the stone's hole at her eye.

'Oh,' she said, and her voice was all surprise. '*Oh*.' She juddered as if she'd been shocked with electricity. Seawater from the inlet rose into a wave, looping round Lily's legs and arms until it burst into a thousand droplets that fell like rain at her feet. 'The voices,' she said in wonder. 'I hear voices everywhere.'

There was a far-off scream, and with a silent cry Autumn was yanked from the cave and dropped outside the Big House. Lily and Isolde, older once more, were crouched beneath a hawthorn tree, watching the rain.

The storm was as wild as Autumn had seen it, but she didn't feel cold. She felt nothing. The rain passed through her skin like mist.

'Wonder if the sea lady is singing at the shore today,' Lily giggled, shivering in her thin dress and cardigan. 'Not sure even *she's* that brave.'

'The sea lady?' Isolde tilted her dark head curiously.

'The one that sings shanties at the waves. Mermaids and that. Anyways, Izzy, we going in or what? My goose pimpleys have goose pimpleys.'

Isolde took a moment to answer. 'So you *do* want

to come in, Lily? You come willingly then?'

'Stupid question, Iz,' Lily giggled. 'Will isn't back from the mainland for an age. I'm bored out of my wits and got a fancy for ginger and sea spice.'

Lightning flashed like an electric shock. Lily and Isolde were swallowed into the blizzard and Autumn was seized by the wind, tossed into the air as if she were nothing more than a puppet.

When she found solid ground again, she was on the cliff. She couldn't see Lily. Or Isolde. The storm was too thick. The waves were higher than mountains. The church bell rang frantically in the gale.

'Lily? Lily!' A distraught shout broke through the noise. A boy – about sixteen – scrambled down cliff steps. He took off his coat and dived in the sea, but a wave carried him away and dropped him back on to the rock.

Find her! Autumn screamed, but her voice was silent.

The boy tried again, but the waves were too high. He lay weakened on the cliff ledge, angry tears streaming down his face. 'LILY!'

There was a muffled scream, somewhere close and yet far away, and Autumn searched desperately for

Lily – but there was nothing except the sea and the storm. From deep within the shadows, the low hum of a song began.

Yo-ho-ho, heave, my lads, the iron, lads, pull it lads
Till it's taut, it's tautened, lads, then let the iron go.

'I'll find you, little one!' the boy cried. 'I'll find you!'

With his promise still echoing, the storm retreated. Autumn was pulled back through fog and time until she was back on her own bed . . . a dead girl peering at her worriedly.

62

The stone rolled out of Autumn's hands and dropped back on to the carpet. She forced her eyes open, but the room was spinning and her head was still halfway between worlds.

'Are you going to faint?' Lily fretted as Autumn slid off the bed. Her eyes were as big as planets. Autumn lay her cheek against the floorboards and tried to ground herself, but her thoughts were a scrambled mess.

Lily was like me.

I know where Will is.

What has this got to do with Dad?

The candle had almost burnt to the wick and the shadows in the room had grown longer. Lily's scent of sand and seawater – horribly fitting, as it turned out – enveloped her like a hug.

'Miss?'

'Oh, Lily,' Autumn croaked. 'Oh.' She wanted to throw her arms round her, to comfort her, but Lily was made of air now. She wasn't the solid, flesh-and-blood girl that had lit up the room.

'What's the matter? What did you see? Was it bad? Did you see how I died?' Lily chewed the end of her plaits, jiggling with worry. Autumn faltered. Perhaps she shouldn't tell her. But then death was so personal. Who was she to keep it hidden?

'I didn't see *exactly*. But I think it was an accident. Lily, I think you drowned in the storm.'

'Oh.' Lily swallowed and sank back on to the patchwork rug.

'And I think Will tried to save you. But he didn't get there in time.'

'Of course, miss. Will would have done anything.' She was unmoving. Staring.

Autumn pulled herself up to sitting so she was next to the ghost, their little fingers nearly touching. The two of them rested their heads against the wall.

'Lily,' Autumn whispered. 'You were like me?'

'How d'ya mean?'

'Your ma. You could see ghosts too?'

Lily paused for a moment, and then something clicked behind her eyes. 'Oh, Ma. Oh. How could I forget? She used to sit on here . . .' She crossed to the bookcase. 'Only this weren't here, it was her old chair . . . and I read her books on my bed over here.' She stood underneath the window and put her palm to the glass, leaving no handprint. 'She got poorly in the war. Then she wanted to stay awhile, keep an eye over us. But she isn't here now, is she? So maybe Will put her stone on a tower after . . . after me. He must have been so lonely.'

Autumn's chest ached. Silence fell in the bedroom, broken only by the island's symphony of thunder and rain.

Autumn looked away. To her dismay, the images of Lily's life were already fading from her mind, like footprints covered by snow. She had to act now. 'I think I know where Will is. But . . . people are fragile. I want to be sure first.'

Happiness ignited Lily's freckled face like sunlight. 'Miss, I couldn't thank you enough.'

'Don't thank me yet.' Autumn took her spotted rain mac from the cupboard and raced to the door. 'Let's just hope I don't forget on the way.'

63

She lurched out of the kitchen door and up the coiled track, not caring that night had fallen or the rain was flooding down the back of her neck. If she hurried, she'd be there and back in ten minutes. She had a bad feeling she wouldn't remember anything of it after that. It was already slipping away from her.

'Will, Will, Will,' she incanted into the darkness, determined not to forget.

Far below, the sea clawed at the cliffs. The mist had well and truly gone, replaced by the worst storm she'd ever seen. It wailed and screamed and battered her face. Autumn dropped her head against it and ran as fast as she could, her breath growing shallower with each step. When she finally reached the Big

House, it was barely visible in the storm. Just a dark, imposing shadow shrouded in rain.

Will, Will, Will.

With a pained squeak, she rammed herself against the iron gate and landed in the Hawthorn courtyard with a bump. She raced to the porch and hammered her fist against the door, fighting through the embarrassment and the shame that she would wake everyone up. She had to do this. For Lily.

The door swung open promptly to reveal Lord Hawthorn still dressed in tweeds. Neptune and Triton peered out from behind his legs.

'Miss Albert,' he said, grey eyes widened in shock. He didn't seem unhappy to see her. Or very tired, either.

Autumn suddenly felt very small and very silly. Like a drenched mouse. She fiddled with her fingers awkwardly, conscious of his mood in the cave. 'I'm sorry it's so late, but Lamorna said I could use the library whenever I wanted.'

A pause, and then he offered her the jolliest of smiles. It made his beard twitch. 'By tide and by moon, what a true Imberian you are to brave this storm for a story. Of *course* you may use the library.

Absolutely, do come in. Allow me to take your coat.'

Relieved, Autumn shook it off and handed it over gratefully. 'I'll be really quick. I promise.'

Lord Hawthorn draped her coat over his arm. 'Nonsense, my dear. You must stay as long as is necessary. I say, Lamorna?' he called up the stairs. 'Would you look who's here?'

Will, Will, Will. The memories were already fading like an old photograph.

'Autumn! What on earth are you doing here?'

To Autumn's relief, Lamorna appeared at the top of the staircase. She didn't look like she was going to bed either. In fact, she looked even more glamorous than she usually did. And very surprised.

'Lamorna!' Autumn grinned sheepishly and shuffled past Lord Hawthorn. 'I'm so sorry. I know it's late, but your dad said I could use your library.' She tried to hide the pool of rain gathering at her feet.

It took a moment for Lamorna to reply. She glanced at her father and rearranged her features into an uncertain smile. 'Why of course, my friend,' she said, beckoning Autumn up the stairs. 'I was just . . . I was just about to call on *you*.'

Autumn skipped up the stairs, past the pictures of

Hawthorns past and on to the rug-draped landing. The lights were off. Flaming orange torches blazed above their heads as though they were in a medieval castle.

'Just a precaution.' Lamorna's cool voice floated behind her. 'In case the electricity is taken by the storm.' She swept into the shadows of the library, leaving Autumn scampering in her wake.

Will, Will, Will.

64

She rushed to the portrait of Lord Hawthorn, hoping her memory hadn't failed her. But no, there it was. The white flower dangling from his hand.

'Oh, Lily.' It was as if a knot had come undone inside her. 'There you are.'

'I was just setting off to call for you, friend.' Lamorna glided across the library to the chaise longue. She sat bolt upright, sounding oddly clipped. 'I wondered if you wanted to stay here tonight. We could have a sleepover in the storm. Tease the waves from the highest point on the island.'

Any other time, Autumn would have been as happy as a pig in mud at this suggestion.

'I'd have loved to. But there's something I have to do. Honestly, I'll be gone in a second.' She traced the portrait with her finger.

'So, you're here willingly then?'

There it was. The artist's signature. Nearly hidden at the bottom of the painting.

W. Emlyn.

'Autumn, what are you doing? Did you hear me?'

'Hmm?'

Will had never been short for William. It was short for Wilfred.

Fred.

The white flower – a lily – painted for the drowned sister he tried to save. His tribute to her. Autumn touched her fingers lightly to her lips and pressed them against the canvas.

I'm so sorry.

When she got home, she'd tell Fred everything. Lily could live in his house. She could tape Jack's card together and ask him to come back. They could all be the Ghost Gang, together.

'Autumn, I asked if you're here willingly.'

There was something about that phrase. What was it? Her stomach tightening, Autumn slunk back from the painting. Where had she heard it before? 'Er, yes. Lamorna. Of course I'm here willingly.' She laughed nervously. She wasn't sure why. 'Thanks a million for your help, but I have to go now.'

Lamorna didn't move. In fact, she just stared at Autumn, her face blank. She didn't look anything like herself at all. An inexplicable icy prickle made its way up Autumn's spine.

'So, I'll just . . . go . . .' She made for the library door, suddenly desperate for home and bed and her ghost friends. The landing was a hair's breadth away when Lord Hawthorn marched in. His pink cheeks glowed.

'Well, isn't this jolly? I thought I'd come and join you both.'

For reasons she couldn't explain, she backed away from him. He was staring at her like she was prey. But these were her friends. Weren't they? She glanced at Lamorna, but the girl remained as silent as the grave.

'Lord Hawthorn, sir, I'd like to go home now please.'

'Oh, child. I know you would.' He slammed the library door shut. 'But I'm afraid that's impossible.'

65

Ten minutes later, and Autumn was sat rigidly on a wooden chair, staring at the two predators opposite her. The library had lost its splendour. It had become blood-red and austere, with a tall ceiling and the dead sea monsters mocking her with their cold eyes. Every part of her was primed to run.

A fire blazed in the grate, the flames wild and long. Lord Hawthorn stabbed it with a poker and came to stand behind the chaise longue, laying a hand on Lamorna's shoulder. He wore a smug smile on a face she didn't recognize. Any resemblance to Father Christmas had long gone.

'Miss Albert,' he began. Even his manner of speaking was different. Slower. Colder. 'I would like to regale you with a story. Oh, tush, let's say *two* stories.

I have been waiting a lifetime for this – I deserve to relish it.'

Autumn's nails dug into her jeans, fear and injustice tasting like bile in her throat.

Lamorna said nothing.

'Many centuries ago, Imber seemed but an empty island off Cornwall's coast.' Lord Hawthorn circled the chaise longue with echoing strides. 'It took four settlers from the mainland to stumble upon it and call it their home.'

Could she run? The door to the library was locked shut. The windows were impossibly high, far too high to jump from. She'd only land on the rocks, anyway.

'But Imber Island was ancient beyond thought, and already inhabited. A sea witch. She welcomed them to her land, curious for tales of humankind.' Lord Hawthorn was clearly hypnotized by his own performance. Autumn wondered how hard it would be to push *him* out the window.

There was a groan from outside, the crash of sea upon rock. The floor shook beneath their feet. Autumn gripped her knees in alarm, but her captor went on, unaware.

'Now, this woman was a water spirit as old as Time itself. A witch with the gift of music who could weave the shore to her will and use her song to call upon the waves. But most mysterious of all, Miss Albert, – and this is where it gets interesting—'

He paused by Autumn's chair so she was forced to look up at him. The firelight cast menacing shadows on his body, rendering him almost demonic. 'This woman could call upon the Realm of the Dead.'

'Realm of the Dead?' Autumn grew hot under his glare.

'Oh, yes,' he said. 'Upon gazing through the hole of a witchstone, the sea witch could talk to spirits as real as you or I. Now, I rather believe there might be the *teensiest* connection here. What do you think, Miss Albert?'

66

Autumn's heart skipped at least seven beats.
What does he know about me?

'I don't know what you're talking about,' she answered, keeping her voice flat. 'Getting a bit bored, to be honest.' She enjoyed seeing his feverish smile fade. Apparently, Mum's side came out in times of extreme stress.

The storm's roar gathered pace outside the window. It banged on the glass and begged to be let in.

Lord Hawthorn regarded Autumn with a thin snarl. 'Playing this game, are we?'

'What game? If it's charades, you're really bad at it.'

A slight whimper came from Lamorna's direction,

but she was still staring straight ahead like a broken doll.

Her father's eye twitched.

'As you wish, Miss Albert. I'll go on. The sea witch fell in love with a settler and bore his child. But the settler grew fearful of his son's power and his time spent with the dead. By nightfall, he took the child to the mainland and told his wife he'd died. That same morning, he left the island for ever.'

'That's so cruel.' Autumn couldn't stop her whisper. Morvoren's song. The woman and her lost child, and Georgy of May. She frantically attempted to connect everything in her head, but her own fear screamed and jangled in her ears.

'Necessary,' Lord Hawthorn answered. 'A man does what he must against the whims of women.' Autumn's hands jerked. She longed to rip his beard off, but he was marching towards the vast window with a theatrical flourish. As if he'd conjured it, fork lightning pierced the ocean.

'Driven mad by the loss of her child, the sea witch swore revenge on the humans that had invaded her home. She cursed the witchstones, cursed Imber and cursed all that lived there. Do penance, or she drowns the island with her tears.'

Lord Hawthorn slunk towards Autumn like a cobra about to strike, his grey eyes locked on hers. 'Lamorna reassured you that our family ensures the island's safety, did she not?'

She didn't answer. Could he hear the hammering of her heart over the rage of the storm?

'Each time the storm comes, the Hawthorn family undertakes a sacred ceremony to keep the island safe. The sea witch demands her child. And to appease her, we offer another.'

Bands of terror wrapped round her torso. This wasn't funny any more. She had to go. Mum would be worried.

Wait.

The day of the swim. The secret doors. The Sea Glass Room. She was small and quick; she could dart out of the chair and run. But no, Lord Hawthorn was by her side once more, bowing his head so he could purr in her ear.

'And here comes my favourite part, my dear.' Hot spittle sprayed her skin. 'Her curse spread through the islanders like a virus. Each generation was doomed to birth a child fated for the flood. A child with the same power as her own. Can you *possibly* imagine who I mean?'

She wished she couldn't.

A child with the same power as the lost son.

Just like Lily.

Just like me.

67

Autumn shot out of her chair like a bullet, but Lord Hawthorn was too fast. He grabbed her arm and squeezed his fingers around it like a vice.

'Alley-oop, dear girl,' he said.

She kicked at him wildly, but he held fast.

He put his spare hand on the wall, and the same door she'd been running for opened at his touch. He dragged her down the spiral staircase, Lamorna sweeping mutely behind with a flaming torch. They landed in the same marine-blue room, the walls of coloured glass closing in on her like the bars of a prison. The storm outside was a muted wail.

Panting, Lord Hawthorn pushed her to the ground in a fierce-eyed heap. Autumn blocked him out and tried to recall what colour glass Lamorna had tapped for the cave. Blue? Amber?

Secret doors are everywhere. You'd never suspect where they are. Much of the sea glass is just sea glass.

Any secret door would do. She just had to hide. The glass was in touching distance and she leapt up, thumping as many as she could reach with her palm.

Nothing happened.

'What a shame,' Lord Hawthorn chuckled. 'All the doors are locked. For now, at least.'

Autumn crawled into a corner and hugged her knees to her chest. The tiled floor burnt ice-cold on her skin.

'And my part as storyteller draws to a close. Lamorna?'

The torch flame quivered in Lamorna's hands, and the sea-glass-covered walls towered in elongated shadow.

'Come, daughter,' Lord Hawthorn said. 'Don't be shy. You played your part so beautifully.'

68

The small room grew airless and thick with the heavy smell of torch smoke. The mermaid mural loomed above them, the painted starfish demons in the darkness.

'Lamorna?' Autumn whispered over her knees. 'What does he mean?'

The sad-eyed girl's perfect features twisted into hatred. But Lamorna wasn't looking at Autumn. She was looking at her father.

When she spoke, her voice was dry sand. 'Autumn swam like the sea was a part of her. She reached Brae's Rock in a matter of moments.'

The swim? That was some kind of test? Through her jumbled brain, Autumn remembered Lamorna's joyful whoops, the happiness she'd felt on the sand.

Her friend. *That was just a test?*

'And she has the music too.' Lamorna gripped the flaming torch so tightly her skin split at the knuckles. 'She sang at the water's edge.'

If she weren't so scared, the hurt would have cracked Autumn in two. All of the times she'd thought Lamorna was her friend, she'd been reeling her in like a fish on a hook.

Any luck identifying our new seabird? Lord Hawthorn's strange question from a million years ago suddenly made sense. *The seabird is in hand.*

She was the seabird.

Jack had been right. *Hornswoggler.* Her chest burnt.

'However,' Lord Hawthorn chimed in, 'nothing happened when you looked through your witchstone. In the cursed ones, it's that very action that sparks the dormant power.'

The voices, Lily had gasped. *I hear voices everywhere.*

'Miss Albert, you failed the final test.'

What? The breath caught in Autumn's throat. 'So, I can go?'

'Oh, my dear, no,' Lord Hawthorn cooed. 'Lamorna found a way.' Something was produced from Lamorna's pocket and before Autumn could cry out in shock, she saw her Bowie-cat notebook held aloft like a prize trophy.

When did she get it?

The beach, after the ceremony. The long hug.

She glared at her old friend, willing her to look at her, to face what she'd done. But she didn't. In fact, Lamorna couldn't seem to see her at all.

'You're an exception to our rule, Miss Albert.' Lord Hawthorn took a pocket watch from his waistcoat, nodded as if satisfied, then pressed a palm to the middle starfish on the mural. A thin door swung open and he reached inside with a grunt. 'Your curse has been with you since the day you were born. I have my own theory as to why, but all in good time.'

Two black cloaks were produced from within, and he offered one to Lamorna who took it wordlessly. The embroidered gold circles winked in the firelight. He draped the other over himself, and in the shadows, Lord Hawthorn was a vampire, a monster from an old movie.

He lunged for Autumn without warning, but she rolled out of his reach and through his legs, not able to see where she was going, only pressing herself against the wall to waste time, any time, as he rounded on her like a wild dog upon a rodent.

He grabbed her arm and forced it behind her until it felt like it might snap in two.

'Walk,' he spat in her ear.

Then the wall opened and they were in pure darkness, surrounded only by the echo of footsteps and the dying flame of Lamorna's torch.

Autumn wanted Mum. She wanted The Dog. She wanted Jack and the radio and her Beatles duvet.

'I promised a second story,' Lord Hawthorn muttered as he pushed her forward and up endless steep stairs. 'Thirty years ago, I had the same task as Lamorna. Befriend the child. Bring him willingly. But he escaped.' His breath shot out in short, angry puffs that hit the back of her neck. 'The flood devastated St Brae's. The islanders were terrified. My mother died of shame. It wasn't my fault.'

They were nearing an open door, lit dimly by a single candle. Autumn's legs buckled.

'We would not survive another flood. But I have atoned for my mistake,' he went on. 'After all these years of searching, I found him. And I brought him back.'

Autumn was shoved into the room. The candle lit the only thing in sight. A giant, wrought-iron cage suspended by a chain.

'I have honoured my family.' Lord Hawthorn sounded giddy. 'The island will be safe once more.'

Autumn's blood turned cold.

Lying curled up inside the cage was a long figure, clad in a knitted jumper and overalls.

Dad.

69

'Daddy?' Autumn whispered.

The figure shifted weakly and lifted his head with obvious difficulty.

'What?' he rasped, before his eyes fell on Autumn. As if possessed, he shot up on to his feet.

'No, NO,' he cried. His hands were tied to the bars, but he kicked wildly with his feet. 'Jago, let her go, let her go now!'

And then, for one of the only times in her life, Autumn began to cry – hot, thick tears that streamed down her face and splashed on to the stone floor. Her whole body was hollow.

'Daddy, you're alive?'

At the sound of her voice, he calmed and wrapped his fingers round the bars. 'Look at me, my darling.

It's just you and me here, OK? Just you and me.'
He turned on Lord Hawthorn, eyes blazed and teeth bared. 'You *swore*, Jago. You swore if I came willingly, you'd leave her alone.'

Lord Hawthorn smiled. 'I lied.'

He dragged Autumn towards the cage. She hacked at his shins with her heel, but he batted her away and reached for a key that hung beneath his cloak on a long chain.

Dad growled like an animal caught in a net. 'I'll kill you, Jago.'

Lord Hawthorn smiled, a thin sneer that spread across his face like oil. The apples of his cheeks looked sunken. 'Oh, Llyr. Nothing can touch me, old friend. *Two* of you. I have more than fulfilled my destiny. You must fulfil yours, too.'

He opened the cage door and pushed Autumn in so she landed on the floor with a thump. 'Not long to go now. Jolly exciting this, isn't it?' He locked the cage door and toddled through the wall. There was one last, lingering stare from Lamorna, before she too vanished.

A jolt of pain shot through Autumn's back, but she shook it off and rolled on to her front. There he was, crouched in front of her, staring at her like she was a ghost too. She was scared to move in case he faded into dust.

'Dad?'

His eyes were haunted and rimmed with purple.

'Dad, are you alive?'

He'd always been so solid, but even in the darkness she could see he was clearly stick-thin. His jumper hung off him.

Skin stinging from the bitter cold, she reached out and put her hands gently on his face. It was such a wonderful face that she'd never thought she'd see again, and she felt the sharp wires of his beard, grown down to his chest. He was warmer than she was, his breath ragged but there – he was breathing.

'My darling,' he said softly, lifting his bound arms as high as he could. She tumbled into him, and even with his hands tied to the bars he squeezed her into one of his bear hugs. It was the most wonderful moment of her life. She buried her face into his neck and smelt a hint of sandalwood and fires and banjo strings and the forest. And just for a moment, everything was all right.

70

When he let her go, they were both crying.

'I don't understand,' she whispered. 'You were dead. We had a funeral. We came to Imber because of your will.'

Dad's face crumpled. 'Oh, my love. Autumn. I'm so, so sorry. The Hawthorns must have faked my death. Forged a will.'

The image of Weltingham, the ghost at the solicitor's office, came to her in a flash. *I need to pass on a message about the new lawyer. It's terribly urgent, miss, please . . .*

'What happened?'

Dad leant his head against the bars. When he spoke, his voice was quiet but steady. 'I've been hiding from them as long as I could remember. It was advertising the tours in Cornwall that did it. It was stupid, but I suppose after thirty years I got complacent. Jago sent a letter. I met him on the beach and he told me that if I came willingly, they'd leave you alone.' He paused, his face half in shadow. 'How much do you know about me? Do you know who I really am?'

Autumn slid under his arm. She still fitted perfectly. 'Lord Hawthorn called you Llyr, not Luke. I saw a picture of you in a book. It said "*L.T.*".'

Dad pressed his thumbs into his eyelids. 'Llyr Trethevy, Autumn. My name was Llyr Trethevy.' The name sounded strange, like it had breathed air after years of being locked away. 'But I'm Luke Albert really, sweetheart. I'm your dad.'

'And Dad . . .' She could hardly bring herself to say it. 'You can see ghosts, too?'

He nodded and buried his face in his hands. 'Since I was five. What you must think. I'm such a coward.'

'No, Dad.'

'Yes. Yes, I am. I hoped so much it would end with me. But when we moved and you started talking about that chimney sweep boy, I knew.' He laughed that wonderful, delighted guffaw that sounded like he'd been taken by surprise. 'He used to watch me eating cheese sandwiches in the laundry room, cheeky so and so.'

'I know,' Autumn giggled. 'He told me.'

Dad peered down at her. The candlelight made his face glow. 'My girl. You are so much braver than I could ever be.'

'No, I'm not. We all hid things, Dad. You, me. Lily. She's a ghost; one of us. We hid parts of ourselves too.'

He kissed her head and she let her breathing fall in time with his. She could just make out the crescent moon blazing through the bars of the window above. Angry clouds churned in a star-strewn sky.

'I ignored the ghosts.' Dad was quiet. She wasn't sure if it was even meant for her. 'I blocked them out. When you stopped talking about them, I thought you'd done the same. Until I saw Jack.'

There was so much she wanted to say. How she wished he'd told her, so she wouldn't have been so alone. How they could have helped each other, and all the lost souls that sought them out. They could have done some real good. But it was all too late now, and it didn't matter any more, so she just shook her head and cuddled up to him.

'How long do you think we've got, Dad?'

He kissed her on top of her head again. 'It doesn't matter, sweetheart,' he whispered. 'We're together.'

71

A ball of fear had become lodged in Autumn's throat. 'Mum won't know the truth, will she Dad?' she managed. 'Only...'

'No,' Dad said firmly, although he scrunched his face up at the mention of her. 'It happens at night, in the middle of the storm. Everyone's either asleep inside, or has already sailed to the mainland to wait out the danger. The islanders, the families – nobody knows anything. An accident. That's all.' He looked away. 'They must've thought the same of me.'

'Wait, that's it!' Autumn bolted up like a jack-in-the-box, startling Dad out of his skin. She couldn't believe she hadn't thought of it. Her voice dropped to a whisper. 'Last time you escaped. Can't you do it again? How did you do it? We can get you untied, somehow . . .'

It was pointless. Dad started shaking his head before all the words had tumbled out of her mouth.

'I did nothing, Autumn. Someone pulled me out.'

'But surely . . .'

'No.' His voice was cracked, but strong. 'That was thirty years ago. He wasn't young then. I don't know who he was, I think he worked here, but he certainly won't be around any more. For all I know, Lady Isolde could've had him killed the minute I left.' He shuddered. 'That's haunted me for decades.'

Autumn sank back down into his arms and let her last remaining hope fly through the bars of the cage.

The storm roared and rattled the barred windows. Autumn thought about Lily, screaming for Will. She thought about Llyr, forced to leave his home and change his name. And she thought that out of all the lost children, she had it lucky really. She wouldn't be alone.

'Dad?'

'Yes, my love?'

'Your beard looks awful.'

'I know.'

There was a noise from the wall and the Hawthorns swept in. Balanced on Lord Hawthorn's shiny head was Lamorna's friendship crown from the cave. It was too small for him and the seaweed had woven loose, making him appear even more amphibian than usual. The hawthorn berries looked like spots of fresh blood.

Lamorna hung more flaming torches from brackets on the wall and looked like she wanted to be somewhere – anywhere – other than there. It only made Autumn despise her more.

The room was filled with a sickening orange glow, and her gut twisted. It lit the chain, suspending the cage from the ceiling and tied to a winch. The cracked grey stone of the wall. The lever, jutting out from it.

What does it release? What's underneath the cage?

She squeezed Dad's arm until it turned white.

'There's nothing to fear, sweetheart,' he whispered in her ear. 'I promise. Just hold tight and close your eyes.'

Lord Hawthorn pressed his reddened nose against the bars, and strands of his beard poked through the gaps. 'Our moment has arrived.' He held crossed fingers in the air. 'Our destinies entwined once more, Llyr. It's an honour, old friend.'

Dad didn't answer. Rage burnt in Autumn's belly. 'Hey, Lamorna,' she spat. 'How does it feel? Knowing that I trusted you? Told you stuff? Feels good to be a murderer, does it? I thought you were my friend.'

Lamorna turned ashen. 'It's nothing personal . . . Mainlander,' she croaked, eyes on the floor. 'It's just tradition.'

Shaking her head in disbelief, Autumn buried herself under Dad's arm. It was like she was floating above all this, watching the scene play out like a film. *This isn't real, surely?*

'Llyr Trethevy and Autumn Albert, you were born fated as the sea witch's sacrifice,' Lord Hawthorn announced, euphoric. His speech dripped with glee.

He reached into his coat and pulled out two witchstones. 'So kind of you to bring both of these, Miss Albert,' he said. 'I'll just hold on to them.'

Autumn gasped. 'They were in my coat. Dad, why does he need the stones? What'll happen to us if he's got them?'

'Nothing to worry about, sweetheart,' Dad whispered. 'I'm here.'

No, it's actually happening.

She pressed close into him, smelling home.

72

I n the blink of an eye, Lord Hawthorn pulled the lever jutting out of the wall and a trap door beneath them snapped open. It was built into a jutting shelf of rock, and Autumn and Dad lurched from side to side as the cage dangled precariously over the hungry jaws of the wild ocean.

Lord Hawthorn turned the winch and fed the iron chain through his hands slowly.

'Father, this isn't right.' There was a cry from the darkness and Lamorna emerged, tears streaking her pale face with silver. 'She's my friend.' She flung herself at him, pulling at the folds of his cloak. 'Stop, Father, please.'

'Lamorna, you're a failure of a Hawthorn and you're a failure of a daughter,' Lord Hawthorn hissed and twisted out of her grasp. 'This is your blood right. You'll watch and you'll understand.'

She collapsed into helpless tears. 'I'm sorry. I can't. I'm so sorry, Autumn.' Her hands clamped against her ears, Lamorna backed through the secret door and vanished.

'Good riddance,' spat her father. 'There is no room for doubters here.'

Dad kissed Autumn's head.

'Hey, sweetheart,' he said, and his voice was wobbly. 'Remember when we went camping? It was the depths of winter. Mum was outside, making soup on a paraffin stove. We had to make sure we got a vegan one, remember? I was playing the banjo. You and Jack were climbing trees, watching the snowflakes dance from the sky and land on your noses, and I was so proud of who you were then, Autumn; I'm so proud every minute to be your dad.'

She forced herself to remember that over and over again until Lord Hawthorn let the chain fly through his hands and they shot through the trap door.

The bell of St Brae's chimed in frenzied rings as they fell. The shock of it made her lose her breath; the freezing rain battered on iron and soaked through her clothes as the cage dived through the air like a swallow. It halted suddenly, halfway down from the trap door to the sea, and swung dangerously in the storm.

For a moment, Autumn wondered if it was all over – if they'd been saved – but there was a *creak* of metal and the cage moved again, juddering slowly downwards. They dangled over the deserted half of the island. The Witchstone Towers. St Brae's. Nobody would see them fall.

Through the shriek of the wind came a familiar, eerie hum. Autumn opened one eye to see a single figure at the tower ledge, arms outstretched to the storm.

Nigh on fainting with relief, she wriggled out of Dad's grasp and threw herself at the bars of the cage.

'It's my friend!' she cried. 'Morvoren! Hey! It's Autumn! Help!' Her words were lost to the tempest, but she was sure the woman was looking right at her.

The cage edged closer to the sea and waves licked at her face, cold and salty. Morvoren's shawl flapped behind her like a scarlet bird. She didn't move. Her face looked different.

'Morvoren! Help!'

Dad pulled her back to him and held her tight. 'It's no use.' His voice was barely audible over the wind.

'But she's my friend . . .'

'No, Autumn, she isn't. She's nobody's friend.'

Morvoren flung her head back. Her song was carried by the wind.

Yo-ho-ho, heave, my lads, the iron, lads, pull it lads
Till it's taut, it's tautened, lads, then let the iron go.

Autumn's hope disintegrated.

Not her too?

There was an almighty splash, and they were plunged into the bitter ice of the sea that snaked its way up her legs and to her chest. It grasped at her lungs and stopped her crying out, and by the time the water crept up her neck and over her head it almost felt warm.

They were submerged but she was kicking, instinctively trying to reach a surface that wasn't there as they were dragged further and further down towards the ocean bed.

There was nothing but a world of dark blue and white, and slowly the edge of her vision started to turn black. Her lungs burnt.

Then came an overwhelming peace. A delicious calm that sank into her bones and lifted her soul, and she felt herself drift upwards towards the warm glow of sunlight. It was like she was being carried.

Hold on.

She *was* being carried. She forced her eyes open against the harsh saltwater to see strong arms in striped pyjamas pulling her through the open cage door, grasping hold of her waist. The arms dragged her through treacle until the surface of the ocean grew nearer and nearer, and she burst through with a splash and a flash of light.

Was she dead or alive?

73

The striped arms lifted her on to wet stone and she lay there, her lungs full and her head throbbing. She tried to lift her hands, arms, anything, but her limbs were too heavy, held down by an invisible force.

Dead or alive?

Beside her came a thump, and then Dad was crouching over her, pounding her chest. She turned her head and water flowed out of her, her lungs emptying and her throat raw.

'Autumn, can you hear me?'

Her eyes stung like fire. The world wobbled and shook and then reformed in front of her, shaping itself into a darkened cave dripping with rainfall, smelling of fish and old seaweed. The cave underneath the Big House. They'd come in through the inlet.

Dad's face came into view, pale and petrified.

'Can you breathe? Can you hear me?'

She tried to nod – *cripes, that hurts* – and pulled herself up to lean on a moss-strewn rock. Her breaths were jagged, painful, but there. *Alive*.

'Dad . . . get out . . . secret door . . . Hawthorn . . .'

'I know. I was here before.'

There was another flash of striped pyjamas and wisps of grey hair, and she saw Dad leaning over a figure lying on the rock opposite.

'It's *you*,' she heard him croak. 'You came back. They didn't kill you.'

The answer was as thin as paper. 'Never knew . . . Jago not bright. Trusted me.'

Dad rubbed a dirty tear from the end of his nose. 'Thank you for my life. Thank you for my baby's.'

'T'were nothing.'

She knew that voice. A rusty key was grasped in a long hand. She'd seen that key on a messy dresser more than once.

'Dad, it's Fred! It's my neighbour!'

Fred coughed a hacking, ancient bark, and Dad leant him forward with a large hand on his back.

'It was him? Is he OK?'

Dad stripped off his jumper and draped it across Fred's chest. 'He's breathing but it's shallow. We need to get him on his boat and sail to the mainland.'

'But his wife . . .' Autumn croaked. 'And Mum . . .'

'We'll collect them. Where do you and Fred live?'

'Brae's View.'

Dad laughed drily. 'Of course, he put you in my old house. My mum must've . . .' He trailed off. 'We're too close to the Hawthorns. Let's get Fred home, get us all into warm clothes and then head to the harbour.' With a tired grunt he lifted Fred over his shoulder in a firefighter's lift. 'Stay close to me,' he warned. 'Don't leave my side for a second, and keep to the shadows. They'll find out we're not in the cage when they bring it up. We've got a while, but not that long.'

The cave had muted the storm. In there, the only sound was the trickle of the rain on to the rocks beneath, the only light from the crescent moon. Her breath burst out into steam as they emerged into the deafening torrent, the cold seeping through her veins.

The sea was a blanket of monsters, groaning and

twisting and winding into tornados that stretched as tall as mountains. Rain was as hard as stone; the wind yanked at her skin and tried to snatch her in its claws. She held her hands over her eyes as she struggled to keep upright, only seeing just ahead of her nose. Could only just keep eyes on the swerving outline of Dad at her side, his shoes sinking into sand as he carried Fred towards the track that led to home.

74

The lights were on in both houses and the frantic figures of Beth and Mum were at the Emlyns' kitchen window – Mum screaming into a telephone, Beth sobbing into a tissue.

Autumn ran ahead and hammered on the door. Within a heartbeat it was flung open.

'Oh, thank *GOD*.' Mum burst into noisy tears and pulled Autumn into the warmth of her stomach. Beth shuffled up behind her, rollers in her hair. 'Oh, no,' she said, the tissue falling from her hand as she saw past Autumn's shoulder. 'Fred.'

With a groan, Dad reached the doorway. At the sight of him, The Dog skidded over the floor and launched himself at Dad, barking like he could burst. Mum lifted her head from Autumn's curls.

'Wha . . .' Her skin turned grey. 'No. *No.* What? Luke? *WHAT?*' She seized Autumn's shoulder with the strength of lobster claws.

'*OOOOW!*' Autumn wasn't sure if she was going to hug him or swear at him. 'Don't pass out, Mum,' she said. 'It's OK. It's real. He's not a ghost.'

Dad pushed past them both and carried Fred into the kitchen. Bracken trotted to her master's side and tried to lick his hand. 'Get down, dogs,' Dad panted. 'Sarah my love, I'm going to tell you everything, I swear, but right now we need to get Fred warm, and then we need to get off this island.'

'Right,' said Mum, nodding her head. She was trembling like a leaf. 'His boat's *The Dozmary*. I'll get my kit.'

There was such a bustle of activity, such a flurry of noise and light and barking as Fred was carried to the sofa, that nobody noticed Autumn slip away. Nobody noticed her slide out of the door and back into the storm, sparking with a new kind of electricity.

She was going to end this.

75

Seaweed had tangled in her hair. Each step was a weighted *squelch* as she darted up the island road and down to the other side. She couldn't stop shivering.

The ocean was wilder than it had ever been. It scratched at the rocks with white foam fingers, waves as high as the Big House. The iron chain was still suspended from the trap-door rock, the cage hardly visible beneath the mess of the sea. Any minute now, they'd realize the storm was taking too long to lift. Any minute, they'd realize the cage was empty.

Above them all in joyous ecstasy was Lord Hawthorn, a toadlike silhouette perched on the Big House balcony.

Hatred curled the edge of her lips.

The eerie hum grew louder. Heart thudding, Autumn held her breath as she crept silently past the towers, but Morvoren didn't move a muscle. She was still in the same position as before, arms outstretched with her silver head flung back. Her eyes were opened wide, unseeing. It was like she was in a trance.

Before she could talk herself out of it, Autumn skidded down the steps to St Brae's, tripping over rock and broken shards of stone. The bell was swaying back and forth at the speed of light, its *clang* growing fainter with each gust of wind. She threw herself inside. The rain had broken through the holes in the roof.

It also wasn't empty.

'*You?*' Her stomach dropped to the flagstone floor.

Lamorna Hawthorn was sat elegantly on the altar. She didn't look surprised.

'Autumn.' She raised an eyebrow at Autumn's dripping curls, her soaked jeans. The pool of seawater trailing behind her. 'Later than I was expecting.'

Autumn could barely speak. With the fear. The hatred. The betrayal. 'How did you know I'd be here?'

The girls stared at each other from across the church floor, like two queens locked in a chess game.

Autumn bit her cheek until she tasted blood. *What if she's been sent to catch me? Is this all a trick?*

'Once you knew what we did here, you wouldn't let it go on.' Lamorna's voice was lower. No tinkling bells now. 'I told you at the beach. You're a good person. Despite what you think of yourself.'

It felt like a lifetime ago.

The floor shook beneath their feet. Lamorna paled and clutched the edge of the altar. 'After I left the . . . the dungeon, I didn't know where to go. I stayed in the Sea Glass Room for a while. Then I heard voices and I saw you and your father and – I presume – the mysterious rescuer in the cave. I've kept silent though.'

There was a groan of water against rock as the waves grew higher.

Autumn forced herself not to run. Keeping her eyes fixed on Lamorna, she crouched down and swept the sludge-drenched flagstones. 'These are the names of the drowned children, aren't they?' Her blue-tinged fingers traced wet etchings on the floor. *Merryn. Tristan. Finn.* Tens of other names, stretching beneath the pews and running to the altar. 'Your family steals their witchstones to keep their ghosts trapped underwater. Not *just* to appease the sea witch but because they're different, right?' Her throat burnt with the injustice of it. 'A virus, your father said. We're not *normal* enough to go on the Witchstone Towers with the other islanders, are we? You have to keep us hidden.'

Lamorna didn't answer. She didn't have to.

'That song about iron. Over and over. Why is iron so important?' Autumn turned it over in her brain, trying to make it fit. 'Iron repels witchcraft and magic; it said so in your spell book.' She paced back and forth, trying not to think about the storm and the girl watching her like a hawk. 'The iron cage does half the work – it was enough to keep Lily in a sort of limbo even without her witchstone, but not enough to keep her trapped for ever. So, there must be *something* else keeping them trapped.' She growled in frustration. 'The answer is in here; I *know* it is. Why was this the only place flooded? Why would their names be here? Why were you there, that morning with your dogs? And why did you know I'd come here?'

Her eyes fell on the altar. With a start, she remembered Lamorna's brief loss of composure the day she and Jack had discovered St Brae's – the pale skin, the flicker of eyes to the back of the church. To the altar.

Of course.

'I knew you'd get there,' Lamorna said, and she looked like a frightened child. 'I wish you hadn't.'

76

Raindrops poured through the broken roof like sand in an hourglass. Time was running out. The flood was a hair's breadth away. Lord Hawthorn would notice they were gone. Autumn's family would be waiting at the harbour.

'Please, Lamorna,' Autumn said. 'Let me have the witchstones. You can't leave their ghosts down there any more.'

A tear ran down Lamorna Hawthorn's cheek and plopped into a puddle beneath her feet. She looked torn in two. 'I . . . these stones have been entrusted to my family for generations. I cannot be the first heir to let them go.'

Despite her rising panic, Autumn forced her breath to slow.

Think, Autumn. Think. What do you know?

'Lamorna, what about your mother?'

Lamorna jerked backwards as if she'd been shot.

Bingo.

'What about my mother?'

'You're not all Hawthorn, are you? You're half . . .'
Autumn left it hanging in the air, hoping that she
hadn't pitched this wrong, that this wouldn't push
Lamorna and the stones further away and back into
the grip of Lord Hawthorn.

Lamorna's answer was choked with sobs. 'Karls-
son,' she said. 'I'm half-Karlsson. Mother was from
Sweden. She *hated* my father by the end. What
he did.'

Autumn edged nearer, catching broken books
and shattered wood with her heels. 'Have you got
family in Sweden, Lamorna?'

'Near a lake.' More tears slid silently down
Lamorna's face. 'My *mormor* . . . grandmother. But I
haven't seen her since I was a girl. Father wouldn't
let me.'

There was a deep rumble like the shifting of furniture, and trickles of water began to seep through the
cracks in the walls. Instinctively, Autumn reached

314

for Lamorna's hand. The other girl did not snatch it away.

'I bet she's *so* proud of you for standing up to your dad,' Autumn said, a bit louder than before. '*I'm* proud of you.'

The slightest hand-squeeze.

'Leave here, Lamorna. Sail to the mainland, fly to the lake and your *mormor*. Find where you belong.'

There was a deathly pause while Lamorna stared at her, unmoving. For a moment, Autumn thought she might have made a terrible mistake, that Lamorna would run and scream for her father. But she didn't. She let her hand drop from Autumn's. Looking suddenly shrivelled in her huge cloak, she slid off the altar.

'They're all yours,' she whispered. 'The newest two are in there too. It appears I'm a talented thief.'

Her heart in her mouth, Autumn lifted the cloth. Underneath the altar was a small dark box. The relief made her legs shake.

She looped her fingers round the handle and dragged it out. It was bumpy and slightly warped, like it was centuries old. The top of it was criss-crossed with iron and rusted at the corners. At her touch, blue electricity *zinged* from the box in sparks.

'It's a strongbox,' Lamorna said, taking a chain from round her neck. 'Ships' captains used them to carry jewels across the sea. But this treasure was more valuable than anyone could imagine.' She handed Autumn the chain. A small, intricate key dangled from the end of it. 'You'll need this.'

Autumn placed the chain round her neck and lifted the strongbox, wincing with the weight. 'See, Lamorna? You *are* a good person.'

Lamorna wiped the tear tracks from her skin. 'Not yet. But perhaps, one day.'

There came the sound of cracking ice. A small fracture had appeared in the stained-glass window and was snaking across the angelic face of St Brae and his outstretched fingers. It splintered into veins through the mysterious blur of red and blue at the far end.

Lamorna's eyes widened. 'The flood is coming. We have to get to the harbour now.'

Autumn couldn't take her eyes from the window.

'You go,' she said. 'I'll get there as soon as I can.'

'Very well.' Lamorna bowed her head and lifted her hood against the rain. 'Then until we meet again, Mainlander.'

'Absotootly.'

With that, the sad-eyed girl was gone.

The embedded shells in the wall shattered with the weight of the storm, bursting out like buttons. Autumn pushed down the reflex to panic; to run as fast as she could down to the harbour and into a boat without ever looking back.

But she had to end it. And the further the cracks spread across the window, the more certain she was.

The young man. The outstretched hand reaching for the azure blue and scarlet red.

The dedication beneath. *He heeded the call of home, but never reached its shores.*

Find me.

The voice at Brae's Rock hadn't been Dad at all. It hadn't even been Lily.

'Right, Autumn,' she said to the empty church, and the ferocity in the echo surprised her. 'Get your bum in gear. Move. *Now.*'

77

Slowed by the weight of the strongbox, she ran as fast as she could out of the church. Waves pulled at her ankles but she stuck her head down and forged her path through the howling torrent and up the cliff steps. With each footstep, the tornado tried to push her back down. There wouldn't be long before the pink sun rose over the horizon, and by then there might be no island left.

Come on, Autumn. The voice in her head was the only thing that kept her going. *Do it for them.*

What little energy she had left was running out. Fast. She pushed away the black dots that clouded her vision and clambered towards the ledge. Through the rain she could see her, framed by the stone towers.

'Morvoren!' she called. '*Please.* I can help you. A single wave does not make an ocean, remember? You're not alone.'

For a moment there was nothing except the diagonal rain and Autumn's fast, painful gasps.

'Little maid?' Morvoren didn't turn her head. 'Alive?' Her voice was soft, despite the menace of her outstretched arms and the storm that swirled from her fingertips.

Autumn's mouth was numb, but she didn't have time to be scared. Not now. She crept as close as she dared.

'You sang me the story of the sea witch. Of her falling in love with Georgy of May and her child dying. You sang it to Lily, too. You wanted us to understand why.'

Arms still outstretched, Morvoren turned her head slowly. Her eyes blazed gold, staring through Autumn like she wasn't there. She wasn't the sea singer any more. She was something much darker.

Autumn stumbled over her words, quaking with fear and ice. 'Dad . . . Dad always said that songs get twisted through the years. My neighbour Fred told me about the hawthorn trees. Some people call them maythorns.'

Thunder exploded. Morvoren bared her teeth.

'His name wasn't Georgy of May, was it? It was George Hawthorn.'

A moan escaped from the back of Morvoren's throat. 'Our child died. He *left*.'

Forked lightning pierced the sea and Autumn's stomach plummeted as she thought of her family and the Emlyns waiting at the harbour, wondering where she was. She took a step closer, and another, her breath bursting out in icy smoke. She was so near now she could feel the heartbreak.

'Some part of you wants this to end. That's why you flooded the church, where the witchstones were. I don't think you want anyone else to get hurt, because you didn't just curse the island, Morvoren. You cursed yourself. Your pain trapped you in this sort of loop, and it's like being a ghost, or . . . or like Fred losing his memory.' Her hand brushed the fabric of Morvoren's shawl and it was as hot as fire. 'Things fade, the past and the present get muddled together and you don't know what's real any more. Generation after generation, you've had to watch children die in your name and it has to stop.'

Morvoren glared at her.

'I. Want. My. Son.'

A flash of scarlet and suddenly Autumn was teetering on the edge of the rock, the iron box clutched in her arms threatening to drag her off the cliff and into the waiting ocean. The sea witch was bent over her, silver curls writhing like snakes in the storm. Autumn mustered up her last ounce of bravery and screamed until her lungs ached.

'I know where he is!'

78

Morvoren tilted her head. 'My child?'

Autumn scrambled back on to the ledge. Her whole body was shaking uncontrollably. 'We have to go to the beach.' Frost bit her bones as the sea witch leant forward and snarled.

'Lie to me and I'll send you back to the ocean floor.'

Autumn was silent with terror as she followed in Morvoren's wake, the weight of the iron box sending spasms up her arms. The sea witch carved a silent path through the storm. Up the steps and down the coiled track of the empty island she seemed to glide.

The islanders had long abandoned Imber. There was nobody left. The lights were off in Brae's View, and Autumn's legs threatened to give way because the storm was too thick to see if *The Dozmary* was still at the harbour or whether they were running around the island, screaming her name. Or whether . . . she shook that thought out of her head. She couldn't think about the flood taking her family. Not now.

Stone turned to sand, and at last they reached the shore. The arched silhouette of Brae's Rock broke through the tempest.

'I do not see my child.' Morvoren's voice was a low threat. 'Why have you brought me here?' She raised her hand, and the sea became a deafening churn of pure white. The wind was so violent that Autumn had to crouch over the strongbox, cradling her head to stop herself being snatched away like a lost feather.

'Your son didn't die, Morvoren,' she yelled. 'George Hawthorn lied. He took him to the mainland.'

Morvoren stumbled backwards, and through the torrent Autumn could see the girl behind the sea witch, broken and betrayed.

'He lied?'

'I'm so sorry!' Autumn could barely hear herself. 'But Brae came back looking for you. He wanted to come home, but he never reached Imber. That's his witchstone, there.' She pointed towards the jagged mass in the middle of the sea. 'He's been calling for you ever since.'

There was no answer. Morvoren lifted her other hand and Autumn stuck her head between her knees, readying herself for the strike.

'Come with me, little maid.' The call was gentle. Autumn looked up to see Morvoren holding out her palm. 'Show me.'

A hush descended, and with the groan of an ancient door the ocean was split in two, drawing apart like the Red Sea commanded by Moses. With the iron box tucked under her aching arm, Autumn took the hand of the sea witch and the two of them trod over pebbles and seaweed towards the giant circle of Brae's Rock, cutting through the storm that raged on either side.

As soon as she neared it, she felt the same unmistakeable tingle she had before.

'He's here,' she said, her tongue thick. She placed her hand on the stone and felt a rush of power.

Focus, Autumn.

She couldn't shake the fear that this would work

the same way as Dad and Lily, that another ghost would appear and lead her on yet another veered path. Morvoren didn't exactly seem the patient type.

She closed her eyes tightly and thought of the boy in the glass window, reaching for his mother's scarlet cloak. The crackling electricity of a ghost-shape the day of the swim. The hand pulling her to safety, stopping her from dying the same way he had. How much he'd longed to come home.

'Find me.' The voice came again, but clearer, and more human.

Autumn opened one eye. Then another. Behind a veil of cloud and smoke, a boy appeared.

Morvoren's cry was a whistle on the wind. 'My *son*.'

He had the green-gold eyes of his mother, and brown hair that curled up at the edges. His robes were the same azure blue as her skirt.

'Mother,' Brae whispered.

Morvoren took him in her arms and held him to her chest as if they'd never been apart.

'You are home now,' she said. 'Home.'

Before a minute had passed, the storm had died and Autumn was alone in the middle of the sea.

79

The sky was a lighter blue, with specks of orange peeking out from beyond the horizon. The sea was calmer too, settling into gentle waves that disappeared before reaching the shore. It was as if the world didn't know what had happened.

Autumn was *so* tired, the kind of tired that twitched limbs and dragged you into the earth, but with a final, almighty *heave*, she lifted the strongbox on to Brae's Rock and hoisted herself next to it.

'Hello?!' she screamed, because she wasn't sure of what else to do. She didn't have the strength to swim back to shore. 'Mum? Dad? Anyone?'

'Autumn!' A familiar voice shouted her name, and a peeling sailing boat curved from the harbour. *The Dozmary*. Dad was steering with one hand on the tiller, and Mum was leaning so far off her long plait skimmed the sea.

Autumn burst into tears at the sight of them. 'Dad! Mum!' She screamed her throat hoarse. 'Over *here*!' She waved her arms until she thought they might break. The boat swung sharply in the direction of Brae's Rock, and she threw herself into it, her shaking legs giving way beneath her. She fell into Dad's arms – a salty, drenched mess.

'Sweetheart.' She could feel his heart racing in his chest. 'Are you OK?' He gripped her head with bony fingers. 'Can you feel your limbs? Are you . . .'

'I'm fine. I think I just need to get w-warm.'

Hot hands wrapped her in a blanket and held her close. She tucked herself inside.

'Oh, honey,' Mum said. 'You're safe now.'

The Dog woofed weakly from the corner of the boat and promptly threw up over the side.

'Where are the Emlyns?' Autumn said, sitting up sharply. 'Are they OK? Fred?'

Mum and Dad exchanged a look.

'They got on *The Cornish Pisky* with another family. Fred's alive.' Mum didn't have to say the rest. *For now.*

The little boat jerked to the side as she slipped her blanket off and wobbled to her feet. 'Mum? Dad and I just need to do one thing really quick, OK? Then I want to tell you everything. From the beginning, I promise.'

Mum gave her shining, brilliant smile and Autumn wondered what it must have been like for her, forever waiting at the edge of her family's secrets. 'I'll be here when you're ready, honey. No pressure.'

'I love you, Mum,' Autumn said. 'You're aces.' She pulled at Dad's jumper. 'Dad? There's something we have to do.'

80

Dad's eyebrows creased, but he helped her stand and followed her obediently to the back of the boat. 'What do you need, sweetheart?'

Autumn took the key from round her neck. 'It's time to end it, Dad. All of it.'

She slipped the key into the strongbox lock, and it turned with a heavy *click*. She lifted the lid. Inside, gleaming like buried treasure, the witchstones lay together, all shapes and sizes, new and ancient, grey, white and brown. Each one, a different time. Each one, a life.

'Are these what I think they are?' Dad sounded both impressed and horrified. 'Autumn, are you sure you know what you're doing? You didn't grow up with this poison. I did. If we get this wrong…'

'It's all over, Dad. None of it means what it used to. Can you help me?'

She could see the fight raging in him, but he shrugged and grabbed a side of the box. 'Ah, I broke the rules years ago anyway. In for a penny, in for a pound.'

They looked at each other, and in perfect unison they tipped the box upside down so the stones dropped into the sea. They water rippled as they fell, sending concentric circles to the shoreline of the island.

A rumble began from beneath the sea's surface. A bubbling of a witch's cauldron. A sapphire light, glowing where the stones had dropped.

'*Look.*' Autumn reached for Dad.

Figures emerged from the water, rising from the deep. As white as the sea's surf, they emerged slowly and floated up into the air like paper lanterns. One after the other, more and more, the sound of children's laughter rising with them.

'They're so young,' Dad murmured. Autumn felt his tears on her forehead.

Pinafores, britches, crinolines and rags. Generations of children lost, of families left behind. The secrecy. The pain the Hawthorns had wrought.

No more.

The further they rose, the more their laughter echoed, until finally they reached the clouds and were nothing more than a sparkle of gold in the rays of the rising sun.

They were home.

'Goodbye,' Autumn whispered.

'Hey.' Dad nudged her and pointed towards the island. 'I think you're being called.'

'*Autumn!*' came the joyful cry. 'Miss, you've done it!'

Autumn choked back a sob. Three figures stood on the rocks.

Lily was tanned and bright, her chestnut plaits brushing her shoulders. She looked alive. A tall teenage boy slid his hand in hers, his auburn hair thick and blue eyes bright. His face was just as open and kind as it had been in life. Bracken was between their legs, her tail wagging at the rate of knots.

'Oh, no,' Autumn cried. 'Dad, Fred didn't make it.'

He gripped her hand. 'I know, sweetheart. But look at him.'

Fred put his hands to his mouth, and his call

reached them across the water. 'Tell Elizabeth I love her, will you?'

Autumn could barely breathe for the tears, but she nodded and clutched Dad's hand as they watched boy, girl and dog float into the air and fade into the new dawn.

81

The moment they vanished, there came a low moan like the sound of a ship's horn.

'Dad, *look*.' Autumn climbed up on to the bow of the boat. Despite the lack of wind, the sea kissing Imber's coastline was twisting into a wave, the moan growing louder.

'Autumn, get back. Get back *now*.'

Dad darted to the tiller and the boat jerked sideways, sending them all to the floor. The sea swelled and groaned, rising into a wave that reached towards the island.

'Everyone got off the island, right?' Autumn yelled as they pulled back, the wave showering them with spray. 'There's no one left?'

'We were the last ones to get on a boat. Everyone

left.' Dad was bright red with exertion. 'God, no, wait. Almost everyone.'

A small, bearded shadow stood perched on the balcony of Hawthorn House, facing the ocean with arms spread apart as if he were calling the wave to him. His cloak flapped behind him like the wings of a vampire bat.

'Dad! We have to go back! Lord Hawthorn's still there!' Autumn tried to grab the tiller from his hands but he held tight, his lips pressed together in something resembling regret.

'Autumn, we tried to get Jago on a boat. He refused.'

'But . . .'

'Luke, get going!' Mum yelled.

A shock of lightning and a rain cloud burst above the island.

'My destiny!' Autumn heard Lord Hawthorn shout into the rain. 'Let me fulfil my destiny, *please*!'

As if it had heard him, the wave reared and wrapped itself round the Hawthorn mansion like a spider weaving its web round a fly. The snake's head broke apart from the island with a mighty *crack*, and the Big House and Lord Hawthorn were plunged into the sea, his final scream of servitude echoing as he fell.

Only Autumn saw the two shadows standing by the Witchstone Towers. There was the slightest tip of a silver head, and mother and son dived beneath the sea, the last strains of their song dying with the rain.

Rest, O Fishermen, and pull up your line
The Sea Witch, she'll catch you, her older than Time.

82

They fell into shocked silence as they approached Sennen Cove.

'It's where Fred sent me last time,' Dad had said. 'Away from the main ferry port.'

The whole thing was like a fever dream.

They pulled into the harbour and Autumn watched Dad moor the boat with expert hands. Only a few weeks had passed since she was last on the mainland. And yet everything had changed. *She* had changed.

The warm air was different here. She'd forgotten that.

Mum lifted her out of the boat and held her like she was a toddler. 'Look, honey,' she said. 'It's a new dawn. And we're all together.' She reached into a bag she'd stuffed at the back of the boat. 'In case this cheers you up,' she said. 'I grabbed your box of bits before we left. This was in there. You used to trundle around playing tea parties with it. I don't know why you loved the old thing so much, but I didn't want you to be without it.'

She produced a tattered black-and-white playing card. Sellotape was lovingly plastered over the Jack of Hearts.

'Oh, *Mum*,' Autumn gasped. 'You don't even ... I can't even ...'

'My eyes were open *some* of the time.' Mum's lips twitched. 'Even if I didn't know what to.'

Autumn waited until she was alone before she called him. Mum and Dad had found a group of villagers and were trying to explain everything in loud, animated voices, so she crept beneath the harbour wall and held it to her lips. She had no idea if it would work, or even if Jack would *want* to see her again if it did, but she couldn't bear the idea of being away from him a minute longer. Facing death was funny like that. It made her realize what was important.

'Are you there, Jack? I miss you.'

In the seconds it took, Autumn convinced herself that she'd messed everything up – that she'd never see him again – but then there was a flash of coal-dark light and her best friend appeared in a cloud of chimney fire.

To say he looked sheepish would be an under-statement.

'SORRY!' they both shouted at the same time.

'No, *I'm* sorry.'

'No, *I* am.'

Jack held his cap out like an olive branch. 'I ain't half missed you, chum. I was so grumpy and snickety with you, stopping you from having pals and that. I was jealous of Lamorna.'

'You don't have to explain . . .'

'No, I do. It ain't fair of me, but cos she gets a part of you I don't, I s'pose. I wish I could do all the exciting things that you do together. But suffice to say, shouldn't have said the things I did. Chums?'

Autumn grinned as wide as the ocean. 'Chums.'

He plonked his cap on his head and ash flew into the sea. 'Hold on. Where are we?'

It felt good to smile. Autumn decided she'd do it a

lot more. 'A lot's been going on.' She stepped out on to the sand and leant back, the wind teasing her curls. 'I'm sorry I took you for granted. You and the whole . . . ghost thing. I know who I am now. And I kind of like it.'

'Blooming excellent,' said Jack. 'Cos I do, an' all.'

'Me three,' came a voice behind her. Dad. He scratched his head awkwardly. 'This is going to take some getting used to after thirty years. But it's good to finally meet you, Jack.'

Jack's mouth dropped open. 'Eh? What the . . . ? Mister Albert, you can see me? And you ain't dead? You're supposed to be dead! Autumn, did you see – he ain't dead?!'

'Oh, chum,' she laughed, and it felt like breathing new air. 'Have I got stuff to tell you.'

So, this was the new normal.

Then Mum and Dad were talking to medics, trying to explain everything and get transport home. They were tangled up in each other's arms. It was kind of disgusting, but she couldn't blame them really. The Dog circled round their legs and periodically stopped to retch, but Autumn swept him up and held him close.

'Still suffering, mutt?' she murmured into his fur. He burped in response and rested his chin on the jetty.

Jack was leaning joyfully into the wind, waving his cap round like a cowboy.

This was her family, starting afresh in their own little world. For the first time in her life, Autumn felt like she was exactly the right person in exactly the right place.

There was so much to do when she got back to London. She'd get her grades back to where they belonged, that was for certain. She'd show Mr Wilson who he was dealing with. She'd find friends who liked her for who she was. Maybe one day, she'd even head to Sweden.

But more than all of that, she had a job to do. She'd wasted enough time wishing for a different life. It was time to embrace the one she had and figure out exactly what she could do. She'd let Christian tell her about the apocalypse and learn science from Mrs Kaur. She'd visit Weltingham and apologize. She'd show Jack the world.

Yes, there were things she had to think about. But

for now, this very minute, she was just a girl at the sea's edge with the wind in her hair. And that was enough.

ACKNOWLEDGEMENTS

This ghostly, watery book has been swimming around my head in one form or another since 2016, and it wouldn't have escaped if not for a lot of extraordinary people. If raising a child takes a village, raising a book takes a country.

Thank you to the life-changer Barry Cunningham, and the astonishing Chicken House team for working so hard on *The Witchstone Ghosts*: Laura Myers, Kesia Lupo, Rachel Hickman, Esther Waller, Jazz Bartlett Love (big one to you for being the first to pick Autumn out of the pile), Liv Jeggo, Elinor Bagenal and Emily Groom-Collis. Special extra thanks to the goddess-like editor Rachel Leyshon for all your wisdom, kindness, understanding and patience with a very anxious author. I loved exploring Imber with you and what you've taught me can't be measured.

To Micaela Alcaino for the frankly stunning cover and artwork. You're a magician. I cried when I saw Autumn for the first time.

To Kathy Webb for the insightful and thorough copy-edits.

To my wonderful agent Lucy Irvine for your thoughtful, calm and kind support both with writing and a bumpy year.

To the judges of the 2021 *Times*/Chicken House prize: Alex O'Connell, Jasbinder Bilan, Sophie Clarke and Layla H. Thank you so much for choosing this strange story on the most surreal Zoom call of all time.

To Debbie Taylor, Joanna Moult, Kiran Millwood Hargrave and the team at Mslexia for making this their 2020 Children's Novel Award winner, just as it was about to go in a drawer. Not only did it convince me not to give up, but you changed the course of this book's life. Mine too.

To my pals at WriteMentor: Melissa Welliver, Florianne Humphrey and particularly the wonder that is Stuart White – without WM, this would just have been another unfinished one on the pile. Never forget the worth of what you do. To Emma Finlayson-Palmer for being the first one to say 'yes' and helping to shape this story in the sparkliest way. To all the Hubsters for being total legends, and all the authors and guests I've had the privilege of chatting to.

To the team at Curtis Brown Creative for opening the door to this world, and to Catherine Johnson for your inspired tutelage. To the Autumn 2019 cohort, particularly The Pinklings: Laura Caputo, Sanam Akram, Carey Camburn, Sara Lilley, Marisa Linton, Gillian Bentley-Richardson and Lucille Abendanon – also the amazing designer of my website. You're all phenomenal writers and even better friends.

To my lovely friend Clare Harlow for inspiring me in this career just as you did in the last. And to Ed Thomas, because you're awesome. To everyone who's read pages and offered advice and camaraderie along the way, including Amy Feest, Alex Atkinson, Poppy Garraway Smith, Adam Lester, Gavin Tangen, Kate Brock, Luke Schreurs, Paul Simon, Emma Pass, Anna Britton (and for 'chum'), Cate Haynes, Tricia Gilbey, Marie Day, Emma Norris and Chrissy Sturt. Special mention to Layla Oates, a writer of beautiful stories who is much missed.

To Hannah Dineen for your brilliant feedback, and to your mum Helen for delivering it so beautifully.

To Uxbridge Library for the smiles and the songs and keeping us in books for four years. To Seth Lakeman, Show of Hands and Fisherman's Friends for inspiring this story with your music and providing the (very unofficial, curated-by-me) soundtrack.

To Anna and Mike Rylance Dobson for everything, but particularly Stanley and the sea, my NCT mums for being the strongest group of women I've had the privilege to know, and to the Preaters, for all the magic and all that you are. Hotbuckle for ever.

To Kate, Alex and the Randalls, for all the help and support and chocolate oranges. Thank you too for the wryneck, and for being the reason I know what a birding tour is.

To my Coates and Jones families, for the stories and the love.

To Peter: there aren't words for everything you've given to this book, to me and to our babies, so I shall just say thank you for Crackington Haven, for the 2020 Easter 'holidays' and for Carboc and Bomas. For the banjo and for the woodsmoke.

To Mum, Dad and Lu – thank you a million times over. I love you and wouldn't be here without you. EXTRA special mention to Mum who has read pretty much every draft since the beginning, when Autumn was Amy, Lily was Lila and I had no idea what I was doing. You're the heart of this, and thank you for having eternal faith.

Last, but not least, Daisy and Bert. Thank you for lending me your names, thank you for being the reason I opened my laptop again and thank you for simply being you. I love you both with all my heart.